Usually I wake up with springs popping inside my head, like I'm in the middle of a pinball game where I'm the ball, and I shoot out of bed and directly to the kitchen where I ricochet around after food until by chance I snatch some toast, then go slamming off the padded stool tops like they were lighted bumpers . . .

'Sad, sweet, hilarious . . . the most absorbing novel for children that I have read in a long time' *Boston Sunday Globe*

'The book's action, like its narrator, is nonstop' *Horn Book*, starred review

www.booksattransworld.co.uk/childrens

Also available, and published by Corgi
Yearling Books:

JOEY PIGZA LOSES CONTROL

# Joey Pigza swallowed the Key

## Jack Gantos

Illustrated by Neal Layton

CORGI YEARLING BOOKS

*For Anne and Mabel*

JOEY PIGZA SWALLOWED THE KEY
A CORGI YEARLING BOOK : 0 440 86433 X

Originally published in the USA by Farrar, Straus and Giroux
First publication in Great Britain

PRINTING HISTORY
Corgi Yearling edition published 2000

5  7  9  10  8  6

Copyright © 1998 by Jack Gantos
Illustrations © 2000 by Neal Layton

The right of Jack Gantos to be identified as the author of this
work has been asserted in accordance with the
Copyright, Designs and Patents Act 1988

*Condition of Sale*
This book is sold subject to the condition that it shall not, by way
of trade or otherwise, be lent, re-sold, hired out or otherwise
circulated without the publisher's prior consent in any form of
binding or cover other than that in which it is published and
without a similar condition including this condition being
imposed on the subsequent purchaser.

Set in 12.5/15.5 Century Schoolbook by
Phoenix Typesetting, Ilkley, West Yorkshire

Corgi Books are published by Transworld Publishers,
61–63 Uxbridge Road, London W5 5SA,
a division of The Random House Group Ltd,
in Australia by Random House Australia (Pty) Ltd,
20 Alfred Street, Milsons Point, Sydney, NSW 2061, Australia,
and in New Zealand by Random House New Zealand Ltd,
18 Poland Road, Glenfield, Auckland 10, New Zealand
and in South Africa by Random House (Pty) Ltd,
Endulini, 5a Jubilee Road, Parktown 2193, South Africa.

Made and printed in Great Britain by
Cox & Wyman Ltd, Reading, Berkshire.

## A Note from the Author

In the United States of America, where Joey Pigza lives and this book was first published, the word 'wired' is a slang way to describe someone who is 'out of control' or 'hyper'. 'Wired' is the perfect way to describe someone like Joey Pigza, who has Attention Deficit Hyperactivity Disorder.

I often visit schools to talk about writing books and I've met a lot of kids like Joey – boys and girls. They are great kids and in every way just as smart and capable as any other kid, except they are 'wired'. There are medications – 'meds' – to help them focus on one task at a time and calm down. Some of the 'meds' work better than others, and some of the kids receive more therapy than others. All of them need looking after.

This book is about Joey and his attempt to get the help he needs so that, as his new friend Special Ed puts it, his problems can be the smallest part of who he is.

Jack Gantos

## 1.

# Off the Wall

At school they say I'm wired bad, or wired mad, or wired sad, or wired glad, depending on my mood and what teacher has ended up with me. But there is no doubt about it, I'm *wired*.

This year was no different. When I started out all the days there looked about the same. In the morning I'd be OK and follow along in class. But after lunch, when my meds had worn down, it was nothing but trouble for me.

One day, we were doing math in class and every time Mrs Maxy asked a question, like

'What's nine times nine?' I'd raise my hand because I'm really quick at math. But each time she called on me, even though I knew the answer, I'd just blurt out, 'Can I get back to you on that?' Then I'd nearly fall out of my chair from laughing. And she'd give me that white-lipped look which meant, 'Settle down.' But I didn't and kept raising my hand each time she asked a question until finally no other kid would raise their hand because they knew what was coming between me and Mrs Maxy.

'OK, Joey,' she'd say, calling on me and staring hard at my face as if her eyes were long fingers that could grip me by the chin. I'd stare right back and hesitate a second as if I was planning to answer the question and then I'd holler out really loud, 'Can I get back to you on that?' Finally, after a bunch of times of me doing that in a row, she jerked her thumb towards the door. 'Out in the hall,' she said. And the class cracked up.

So I went and stood in the hall for about a second until I remembered the mini-Superball in my pocket and started to bounce it off the lockers and ceiling and after Mrs Deebs in the next class stuck her head out her door and yelled, 'Hey, cut the racket,' like she was yelling at a stray cat, I remembered something I wanted to try. I had seen the Tasmanian Devil on TV whirling around like a top so I unbuckled my belt and pulled on the end really hard, as if I was trying to start a lawn mower. But that didn't get me spinning very fast. So I took out my high-top shoelaces and tied them together and then to the belt and wrapped it all around my waist. Then I grabbed one end and yanked on it and sort of got myself spinning. I kept doing it until I got better and better and before long I was bouncing off the lockers because I was dizzy too. Then I gave myself one more really good pull on the belt and because I was already dizzy I got going really fast and began to snort and grunt like the Tasmanian Devil until Mrs Maxy came out and clamped her hands down on my shoulders. She stopped me so fast I spun right out of my shoes and they went shooting up the hall.

'You glue your feet to the floor for five whole minutes or you can just spin yourself down to the principal's office,' she said. 'Now, what is your choice going to be?'

'Can I get back to you on that?' I asked.

Her face turned all red. 'Five minutes,' she said. 'Settle down for five, and you can rejoin the class.'

I nodded, and when she was gone I wrapped the belt and laces around my middle and gave it a good tug and began to spin and spin and slam into the lockers and I got going so fast the gum I had under my tongue flew out and my Superball slipped out of my hand and went bouncing down the hall and I kept going and going like when you roll down a steep hill and before long I was bumping on the glass walls around the principal's office like a dizzy fish in a tank. Then the principal came out and pinned me against the wall and we had a little talk about my behaviour goals and I spent the rest of the day on her office floor sorting out all the used crayons that the kindergarten kids kept in big plastic tubs until I had separate piles of blue and green and red and yellow and you know the rest.

## 2.

# Family Tree

My dad ran off when I was in kindergarten and my mom went after him. My grandmother raised me until this past summer. That's when my mom finally stopped trying to get my dad turned around and remembered about me. One morning she rang the doorbell.

'Who's there!' I yelled, and when Grandma and I yanked open the door a stranger was standing on the porch mat, like one of those church ladies dressed in shiny shoes and a Sunday hat.

'I'm sorry for being gone so long,' she said.

'I'm sorry you're back,' Grandma snapped,

and shoved me out of the way with her elbow, which nearly jammed my Tootsie Pop down my throat.

'I just want to smooth things out,' said the lady who was my mom.

'I've heard this all before,' Grandma shouted, and shoved me back again because I kept sticking my head around her hips so I could see what was going on.

I really wasn't sure what either of them was talking about because I didn't recognize the lady. Then she pushed the door open and took one big giant step right into the living room before anyone told her she could. 'Hi, Joey,' she said. 'I'm your mom.'

When she reached out and tried to touch my head I ducked away and said I wasn't sure she was my mom because I didn't even remember what she looked like. She got an awful pain across her face and I figured she must be my mom because no stranger would have been so hurt by what I'd said. But she didn't crumble. Instead she started walking all through the rooms, just shaking her head at the way Grandma and I kept things.

'Now that I'm back,' she said, 'things are going to change around here. No more living in a pigpen.' Then right away she started making up new rules and trying to take control of me and Grandma and the house. I didn't like her at all, and during those first weeks she was back we all fought pretty well.

I was a wired-up mess by the time Mom came back to live with me and Grandma. By then everyone thought my grandma was the nutty old lady responsible for my bad behaviour. But I am how I am because Grandma was born wired, and my dad, Carter Pigza, was born wired, and I followed right behind them. It's as if our family tree looks like a set of high-voltage wires strung across a field from one steel tower to the next. Grandma all the time said I was just like my dad, 'bouncing off the walls twenty-four hours a day.' But he hasn't yet bounced in our direction so I guess he is still bouncing around somewhere else. Grandma said he bounced over to Pittsburgh. But someday he might spring back and just bounce right through our front door. I wish he would because I only just hear about him now, and I'd like to see for myself what he is like. I have one of those wind-up cars with twisty wheels that when it bumps into things can change direction and bump into something else over and over. When I play with it I always think my dad is steering, eyes spinning in his head and his foot all the way down on the accelerator. My toy car gets drained and stops, but I'm guessing that he never winds down. He just keeps on smashing into buildings and signs and parked cars.

I figure we have a lot in common because once when Grandma was in a sudden good mood she said to me as a helpful warning, 'Joey, I want you to pull your act together. You don't want to turn out like your father, do you?'

'Can I get back to you on that?' I yelled as I tried to run off.

'Listen to me,' she said, grabbing me as I ran by. 'Your dad's such a nervous wreck he couldn't stand still long enough to line up for free medicine down at the clinic.'

Then Grandma held me by the ears and I lifted my feet off the floor until I wiggled like a snake and screamed and she let go.

People who blame Grandma for my behaviour are unfair to think that she was really the crazy one and I was innocent. It was more that we were whacked-out partners. We zipped around the house and slapped at each other like one of those World Wrestling tag teams. I'd be the Hulk and she'd be Doctor Doom and when the phone rang we'd run at it screaming and yelling and slam into each other, and by the time one of us got the upper hand the person on the other end had freaked out and hung up. And nothing in the house was ever finished or cleaned up. A jigsaw puzzle of ancient Egypt outlined the dining room table, with the extra pieces piled up like pyramids spilling over onto the floor. I had stacks of homework I had forgotten and drawings of my grandmother's face on big locust bug bodies all taped to the floors as if she'd been squashed by a truck. I stuck wet leaves over the windows, glued my stuffed animals to the chairs, hid all the oven knobs in the dead plant pots, and made huge string spider webs between the door knobs and ceiling lights and floor vents. Every now and again I'd catch Grandma in a web and she'd get tangled up.

'Help meeee. Help meeee,' she'd squeak like the fly with the human face in that crazy bug movie. Sometimes she could be funny. But not often.

Most times she'd just get mad and keep after me non-stop and complain about everything I did.

'Don't touch. Don't wiggle. Don't run. Don't yell,' she'd bark out.

No matter what I touched or said or did, I felt like I was in cartoon hell standing on hot coals with little red devils poking me in the bottom with pitchforks as I jumped from one fiery place to another. Even the words I spoke scalded my tongue. And if by accident I'd sit still for a minute and just vibrate, she'd complain anyway. She could yell at me and knit at the same time. She'd get those needles going as if she were fighting off the Three Musketeers all at once, and before long she'd have a strip of wool that could reach around our block of houses and be tied in a bow. But it never amounted to anything. Everything started became nothing finished, and all her projects and my homework and hobbies just ended up in piles collecting dust.

Even now my bedroom still has the walls painted in Placid Pink where she had got going on the bottom but didn't finish at the top. Someone told her the colour pink would calm me down. But it didn't work.

Until Mom returned my bed was pushed over in the corner along with the chair and splintered dresser drawers with the peeled-off fake wood grain. Old newspapers were spread over the sheets to keep off paint but I'd been using them as a blanket. Sometimes I think if Grandma had finished painting that pink on everything I might have calmed down. I used to sit in my closet and pry open the paint can and stare into the shiny pink circle and was mesmerized for hours. Or maybe just minutes. I could never tell. But if you believe a colour gives off a feeling then I think it is true that pink gives off lots of calm. Maybe that pink just wasn't pink enough because before long I'd turn into my wired self again.

After Mom came back this past summer and started to organize things Grandma got worse. She got meaner and I think it was because she didn't like rules either. I had to stay with her when Mom was at work, and she began to scare me. About a month before school started she was mean all morning as usual and in the afternoon, instead of settling down to knit, she kept getting meaner and meaner. Finally, she got so mad at me for bouncing around she threw everything out of the refrigerator and yanked out the shelves and flung them across the floor.

'Now get inside and stay inside,' she said with the ketchup bottle still spinning around her feet like a bowling pin.

That slowed me down. I looked at her, and her dentures were pulled over to one side and snapping like she couldn't control them, like they could climb up the side of her face and bite her own ear off.

'In!' she shouted. 'Get in before I blow a fuse.' A hot steamy sound came out with each word.

'Don't make me,' I said, hopping from foot to foot. 'Don't.'

'In,' she said and her body snapped like a whip. 'I said get in or I'll tell your mom you won't listen to *my* rules.'

But I wouldn't get in. I knew there were good rules and bad rules, and having a time-out inside a refrigerator was a bad rule.

'Lousy no good kid,' she said, slamming the door. 'I need a break.' She turned and marched outside to smoke a cigarette while sitting in the porch rocker. In a minute I heard her get after someone about throwing trash in our yard and then she stomped off. When my mom came home that night from work I was alone and scared. She saw the kitchen all in a mess and I told her what had happened.

'No wonder you're a nervous wreck,' Mom said. And she was angry. We went looking for Grandma and found one scuffed-up shoe down by the corner sewer grating and that was all. After Mom thought about it she said, 'Grandma was probably so wired she slipped right down into the sewer and was washed away for good.'

We never did call the police, and for a couple of days I kept bending down over the iron grating and cupping my hands and shouting into the dark hole, 'Grandma! Grandma! I forgive you! Come back!'

She never answered and I was sorry because I was the same as her at times when I lost it.

'Grandma isn't exactly like you,' Mom said to me after I told her I was sad. 'The difference is she's more active in the mouth, and you are more active in the feet.' Grandma was always saying the wrong hurtful things for half the day, then she spent the other half of the day apologizing. 'She has a hyperactive mouth,' my mother said. 'You know how sometimes you can't stop moving your feet or swinging on the doors or jumping on the bed?'

'Yes,' I said, hanging my head and scratching at the dry patch on my scalp that I had already rubbed bald and a little bloody.

Mom pulled my hand away and held it between hers. 'Well, your grandmother can't help but say things like, "You don't know what you're doing. You're ruining everything. You never listen to me. I always said you were dumb as dirt."' Mom was right. Grandma would just get so excited about being mean that one thing would lead to another and another, and before long she didn't know what she was saying but her lips were flapping a mile a minute. Then when she finally settled down she would feel bad.

'I'm so sorry,' she'd begin. 'I never knew anything I said upset anyone. You all shouldn't listen to me. You know I'm just a nasty trash-talking old fool.'

She'd say the same thing over and over again. She should have been on meds too. Big-time Grandma-sized meds. But because she was a grandma, people didn't think she was sick. They just called her a batty old bird. But she was sick like me, only old, so her sickness was different.

Now all that's changed since Mom came back, and I couldn't live without her because she's really the one who understands how I am when I get worked up into a wild spell. Like yesterday before school when I was playing stuntman in the early morning. I was diving from the top of the stepladder Mom had left up to change the burnt-out ceiling lights. I belly-flopped onto the couch, then bounced onto the floor. She woke up and in seconds pinned me down and pressed her face to mine and said, 'So what's up, Doc? You gonna be even or odd today?'

'Can I get back to you on that?' I said, trying to squirm away. Then suddenly she held out both fists in front of me. 'Pick one,' she said. I did, and my pill was in her hand. It is always in her hand, like she is some kind of magician.

'See,' she said calmly, and stroked my head. 'You know how to choose what's good for you. So, are you going to put the ladder away?'

'Yeah,' I said, laughing, and got to my feet. I swallowed my pill without water and could feel it roll, then stumble, then roll a little more, then stumble all the way down my throat and vanish into my belly. Then I picked the ladder up and darted across the room, but my aim was off and I slammed into the doorframe. That jarred me. Then I tried it again and again until I nearly had all the paint chipped off around the dented woodwork, and she just let me keep on trying until finally I got the ladder and the opening lined up just right and stumbled through and ploughed into the kitchen table and knocked the plastic rooster salt and pepper shakers to the floor.

'Even when you were a baby you had a hard time getting a square peg into a square hole,' she called out from behind me. 'Remember rule number one: Slow down and think about what you're doing.'

Mom is big on rules for me.

# 3.

# Handful

Over the summer, there was a big meeting about me at school. Mom came home very serious and sent me to my room while she read my file. After she read it she opened my door and sat down on the edge of my bed. She said I should have been kept back a year and given extra help, but no teacher wanted to risk getting me two years in a row.

'I guess I can't blame them.' She sighed. 'You are a handful at times.'

'I don't get how they think I'm such a pain,' I said to her. And I didn't, because most of the time I wasn't even in the classroom. I was in the principal's office, or with the nurse, or I was helping out in the library or cafeteria, or running laps out on the playground. It wasn't like I was a *pain* all day long. Like when it rained the teachers all asked *me* to run out to the parking lot and roll up their windows. I didn't hear them complain when I came back dripping wet. Or if a stack of new supplies was dropped off and I was in the office then I always helped move them into the storeroom and received an 'awesome kid' stamp on my hand, not a 'pain-in-the-neck kid' stamp. Plus I was famous for snatching flies right out of the air, killing all the classroom spiders, and making sure the white mice were always in their cage. I'll bet helpful things like that were not written down in my file. I know I'm not perfect, but I didn't think it was fair that they told me one thing and wrote down another.

'Hearing stuff like that about me makes me sad,' I said to Mom.

'Well, it should,' she replied. 'But this year we can start over. The school wants me to take you down to the doctor and get you fixed up.' Then she reached out and grabbed me and kissed me all over my face and I had to close my eyelids otherwise she would have kissed me right on the eyeballs.

Mrs Maxy had also read my file. When I arrived in her class she assigned me my seat and said that she was going to give me a fair chance to show just how good I could be. And all that first day she kept glancing at me with the 'I got my eye on you' look. I was used to people keeping an eye on me, especially after last year, when a special counsellor was called in to follow me everywhere. He gave me tests and kept sending reports home to Grandma, which she called junk mail and threw in the trash.

I had taken my special meds at breakfast and they were working well so I was mostly sitting still, looking right back into Mrs Maxy's eyes and shouting out the answers when we did our math.

Before lunch my seat felt like any old hard seat, and I felt like any old kid. But after lunch I felt as if I was sitting on a giant spring and it was all I could do to keep it from launching me head first up into the ceiling. My morning pill was supposed to last all day but it let me down. I gripped the bottom of my chair and held tight and watched the second hand on the clock sweep round and round. And it wasn't that the important stuff Mrs Maxy had to say went in one ear and out the other. It was that it didn't go in at all but just bounced off. And when the bell rang I loosened my grip and blasted off for the door.

But Mrs Maxy was waiting for me.

'Not so fast, Joey,' she said, and snagged the back of my shirt collar as I ran by. 'We need to talk.'

That's when she sat me back down and told me about *her* rules. I had to stay in my seat, she said. No running, no jumping, or kicking. Keep my hands on top of my desk. I wasn't allowed to look over my shoulder. No touching the person in front of me. No fidgeting and no drawing on myself. And I absolutely wasn't allowed to say anything until I raised my hand and was called on.

She had all the rules printed out on a little white note card. 'Now these are my basic rules,' she said to me, and taped them firmly to the upper corner of my desktop. 'They apply to *everyone* in the class. I make no exceptions. So if you work by these rules and keep your mind on your studies, then you and I will not have any problems.'

Problem was, I wasn't listening. She had on bright red nail polish and I couldn't get my eyes off the way her fingers tapped on my desktop and were leaving tiny half-moon dents in the wood. And the next day I sure didn't remember a thing she said, and by lunchtime my meds had worn off again and I was spinning around in my chair like it was the Mad Hatter's Teacup ride at the church carnival.

'Joey,' Mrs Maxy said, 'will you come up to my desk please?'

I did. I stood before her and hopped from foot to foot as if I had to pee.

'You're losing it, Joey,' she whispered, and set one hand on my shoulder to settle me down. 'Remember the rules?'

'Rules?' I asked, kind of lost.

'Didn't we have a talk yesterday?' she asked.

'I'm a little antsy,' I said. 'I get this way and I need to do stuff. My grandma used to give me a broom and make me sweep the sidewalk all the way around our block.'

Mrs Maxy shook her head back and forth. 'Well, we already have a janitor,' she said.

'But I've got something you can help me with.'

She gave me a box of used pencils to sharpen. Everyone else was doing some old social-studies handout about presidents. When I got to skip it and just sharpen pencils our class president, Maria Dombrowski, gave me a look. I figured she was jealous because in less than a week I was already the teacher's pet and got to do all the fun stuff. I just crossed my eyes and kept going.

I stuck the first pencil in the sharpener and began to turn the crank. I loved the sound of the wood and lead being ground down. I lowered my nose to just over the sharpener and sniffed the clean smell of wood shavings, which smelled like the inside of my mom's blanket chest where I used to hide from Grandma then pop up and scare her bloodless. I just kept turning the crank and pushing in the pencil and finally I had it ground down to just above the eraser. I pulled it out and checked the tip. Sharp as a needle. I put it in the box and got another and began to grind it down. When I finished that I found a couple of pieces of chalk and sharpened those down so that when I stuck the flat end up between my upper lip and gum they hung down like fangs. Then I saw some Popsicle sticks on the art cart that were used to make paper puppets. I made sure Mrs Maxy wasn't looking, then grabbed one and stuck it in the sharpener. I began to turn the crank, but it didn't turn so well and finally it jammed up and I couldn't get the stick out. I nervously glanced at Mrs Maxy and luckily she was busy stapling all the presidents' heads on a bulletin board. I yanked at the stick again but it was really stuck and I only ended up with splinters in my hand.

I wrapped the bottom of my Pittsburgh Penguins hockey jersey around it and tugged with one hand and turned the crank with the other. The stick came loose and I stumbled back against an empty desk and my fangs fell out and rolled across the floor in pieces.

Mrs Maxy looked over at me and so did everyone else. 'Joey,' she asked, 'is there a problem?'

The question made me feel jittery. I picked up my fangs and stood real still.

'No, Mrs Maxy. No problem,' I said in a small mouse voice.

She nodded, then turned her back on me. But Maria kept frowning at me and then she pulled out a little pad from her desk and wrote down four letters I couldn't see but figured spelled J-O-E-Y. As class president, it was Maria's job to make sure everyone had good behaviour or Mrs Maxy would take minutes off our break time.

Teacher's pet, I thought, then forgot all about her.

The sharpener had a bunch of holes for different-sized pencils, like a regular hole for ordinary pencils, then when you turned the dial there was a bigger hole for thicker pencils, and even a hole big enough for one of those giant clown pencils that are about as thick as my finger.

Mom had said I needed to cut my long finger-nails back because I was scratching myself all up in my sleep. Plus, I thought it would be cool to grind my nails down to sharp points and look like a vampire. So I stuck my little finger in and gave it a good turn but in an instant I jerked it out and started shrieking.

Mrs Maxy spun round and ran towards me.

'I slipped, I slipped,' I hollered. 'It was an accident.'

'Let me see that,' she said, and grabbed my hand.

I held my finger up in the air and it was only a little scratched up and bloody on the tip. But the nail had been yanked over to one side and was just hanging there like when you peel the shell off a shrimp.

'It doesn't hurt,' I said, trying to get my hand away from her and shove it down into my pocket where no-one could see it. 'It's OK.'

The next thing I knew Mrs Maxy had a wad of tissues around my finger and she held it tightly with one hand and told me that it was going to be all right, and she held my elbow with her other hand to settle me down because by then I was swinging round and slapping at my leg with my free hand as if red ants were biting me all over.

'It's not good to hurt yourself,' she said calmly.

'I was just playing vampire,' I explained.

She took me directly to Nurse Holyfield, who said she'd seen worse and not to worry, other kids had done the same. She fixed me up with a big white bandage around my finger so that it looked like a stick with a huge wad of cotton candy on the end.

'The nail will fall off,' she said. 'But don't worry. You'll grow another.'

'Is there a fingernail fairy?' I asked her. ''Cause if there is I'll put it under my pillow and get a dollar.'

She smiled at me, glanced up at Mrs Maxy, and nodded like they both knew something about me I didn't know. People were always giving each other secret looks around me. But I didn't care. I had private thoughts of my own that I didn't share with them, so it made us even.

After class that day Mrs Maxy was waiting for me at the door. 'We have to have another talk,' she said. 'Let's sit down.'

I stared at her because I wasn't sure what to talk about and if I started talking first it could be about anything. So I waited, and she went first.

'Joey, you have to listen to me carefully,' she said in a calm radio voice. 'I want to help you, but you have to help yourself too. Today you hurt yourself . . .'

'It was an accident,' I shouted, and jumped to my feet. But she just put her hands on my shoulders and slowly pressed me back into the chair.

'But you did it,' she said. 'Other kids would

not have and this is my concern. That you don't know what will hurt you or not. And no-one at the school wants to see you hurt. And . . .' She stopped for a moment to be really careful. 'And no-one at the school wants to be hurt by you.'

'I wouldn't hurt anyone,' I said.

'Not intentionally,' she replied. 'Not on purpose. But we have to make sure you don't.'

I don't know why I couldn't listen to her. She talked some more about the dangers of hurting people, but it was as if all her words were crowded up together in a long line of letters and sounds that just didn't make sense. It was more like listening to circus music than to talk.

'Joey,' she said, 'you need to know that there are limits in the classroom. And if you can't live by the class rules then we'll have to send you down to the special-education class for extra help. We've talked to your mom about this.'

'OK,' I said, only saying the word because agreeing to stuff was the best way to make it stop. 'OK. OK,' I repeated. 'I get it.' But I didn't get it because the special-ed room was new and I didn't even know what it was yet.

'Please do *get it*,' she said. 'We all want to keep you going in the right direction.'

When Mom returned home from work I told her about my day and showed her my finger. She sighed, pulled her hair back into a pony-tail, and snapped a rubber band around it. 'Let me see,' she said, and unwrapped my bandage. While she looked at my finger I looked at her face, which turned sad. 'It's gonna be OK,' she whispered, as if loud talk would wake up the hurt.

'I think so too,' I whispered back. Then very carefully she rewrapped the bandage.

'Did you get into trouble?' she asked.

'Not really,' I replied. 'The nurse said it was no big deal.'

'Good boy,' she said, and gave me a air kiss. 'Now, mix me *my* medicine. The beauty parlour was a zoo today.'

I ran over to the kitchen cabinet and got the jug bottle of Amaretto with the red $23.99 price sticker right on the paper label. Mom had been calling it her medicine ever since I got my medicine. I think in the beginning she called it that so I would not feel bad about having to take something to make me feel better. Like we had something in common, because, as she said, her medicine makes her feel better too.

I first got my meds after Mom had her school meeting and took me to the clinic. I spoke with a doc who had a lot of forms and asked me questions like 'Can you do homework while watching TV?' and 'During dinner can you keep your napkin on your lap?' Then he gave me a Rubik's Cube and timed how long I played with it until I gave up. He wanted to know how I felt when other kids called me names, and I asked him how he knew kids called me names. And he said he was just guessing. And I told him some kids on my street called me 'Zippy' because I was skinny and hyper, and other names too, and I didn't like it. Then he spoke with my mom for a long time and made her fill out a lot of forms.

But we must have passed the test because afterwards we went directly to the pharmacy. And while I waited for the prescription to be filled I picked the cotton stuffing out of an old padded chair. By the time Mom gathered her things up and paid for the big bottle of pills, I had hidden all the cotton in my trousers which made me bunchy around the middle, like a lumpy scarecrow. All the way home in the car Mom had borrowed I kept picking it out of the tiny hole I had worked in my pocket and slowly tossing it out the window. By the time I got home I was so scared, because I thought the pharmacist would discover his skinny chair and follow the little wads of cotton to my house, like when Hansel and Gretel first made a trail home with breadcrumbs. I was so afraid I told Mom what I was thinking, and she held my cheeks in both her hands and kissed my face and said, 'Don't worry so much. Now let's get you some medicine.' She put a pill in my one hand and a glass of water in the other, but before I could take the pill she said, 'Just hold on a minute more.' She got the bottle of Amaretto and mixed it with some Mountain Dew and then said, 'See, Mommy has her own meds. It comes in a bottle.' Then we clinked glasses and I took my pill. I was so happy to take it. I could feel it going down my throat like a little white round superhero pill on its way to beat up all the bad stuff in me. Everyone said it would help.

And it did. That first day I felt quiet as a lamb and went to bed early and didn't wake up until the next morning at ten. By then

Mom had already gone to the beauty parlour and left me a pill to take and a note telling me to just stay indoors all day. So I stayed home and felt like a normal kid for a while. But then my old self started to sneak up over me. After watching *Wheel of Fortune* and a *Simpsons* rerun on TV, I got up and made a huge peanut-butter mess in the kitchen, and when Mom came home she freaked and gave me another pill, but already it didn't work as well and I could hardly sleep that night. In fact, after that first day the pills only worked on and off. I never knew which it was going to be. 'Peace or consequences,' Mom called it. She phoned the clinic and a doctor said it was because I was going through extra-early puberty, so my blood was half boy and half man and the medicine worked well on the boy and not on the man. I told that to Nurse Holyfield today when she was fixing my finger, and she said it was pure nonsense and that the problem was we were given the cheap medication and some worked and some were duds.

When I finished mixing Mom's drink I put the Amaretto away and carefully carried the drink to her. She tasted it, then said, 'Joey, if you slip any more, school just might let you slip away like water down a drain and the class will continue on as if you never existed.'

'Is that what happened to Grandma?' I asked.

'Not quite,' she said. 'As it turns out, your dad was in town and Grandma decided it was easier to live where she could do whatever she wanted and nobody would care. So she's back in Pittsburgh with *him*.'

'I hope she's OK,' I said.

'Don't worry about your grandma,' she said. 'She's as tough as old whip leather and might just crack some sense into your dad.' She smiled after she said that.

# 4.

# Go Fish

I was sitting at my desk after lunch and Mrs Maxy had her back to us and was writing a long list of spelling words she had taken out of *The Great Gilly Hopkins*, which was so good I actually could listen to it for more than a minute at a time. But now that I had heard it all I was playing with the house key that was on a long string round my neck. I loved touching that old brass key with the smooth round top that looked like a tiny face. It was like touching something magic. I didn't know how it locked and unlocked doors, it just did. Mom had given me the key since my grandma wasn't around and I got home from school two hours before she got home from work. She trusted me with the key, and we had a rule that I went directly home and once inside I could do anything I wanted except light the gas stove, take a bath, make joke phone calls to strangers, or throw the baseball at the walls, because it dented them. And once I was in the house I was forbidden to step outside or open the door for strangers. This was OK with me because like I'd told the doctor the kids in my neighbourhood were pretty mean. Once a few of them caught me on the way home from school. A kid named Ford held me down and tied a leash around my neck. 'Roll over,' he hollered, and I did. 'Play dead,' he ordered. That scared me and I jerked my head out of the leash, which ripped one of my nose holes so that it bled. But I got away. Now I don't open the door for anyone.

I was messing with my house key and before long I had it in my mouth and I was playing a game. I was trying to train myself to swallow the key so I could slowly pull it back up from inside my belly, up my throat and into my mouth, like I was fishing for bottom feeders. It hurt to do it because sometimes the key got caught sideways down my throat, but when it did that I just gave the string a tug and straightened it out. The only other problem was that every now and again it made me gag so hard I almost threw up.

Since I was doing it after lunch, I thought it would be especially colourful because bits and pieces of food would stick to the key and around the string and I'd suck them off and reswallow them.

Mrs Maxy must have turned round but I never saw her. I was still fishing and wondering if I could pull my liver up, or my kidney, or some organ we had studied in science when suddenly Mrs Maxy swooped down on me. With one hand she yanked the string out of my mouth, which really hurt because the key was about halfway down my throat. Then with her other hand she took her sharp 'teacher only' pointy scissors and cut the string off the key and put the key in my T-shirt pocket.

'Keep your mind on your work,' she said, tapping the rules sheet on my desk. 'Now sit up and listen.'

'OK,' I said, and quickly sat on my hands. As soon as she left I pulled an old photograph of me out of my jeans and set it on my desk. It was a picture of me standing very still with my hands by my side and my eyes looking directly at the camera. I looked like a little statue. It's a wonder a bird didn't land on my head for a rest.

'See,' Mom said, when she gave the photograph to me. 'This is proof that you can be still. So whenever you feel out of control, look at this picture and it will remind you to calm down.'

I looked at the picture and stared into the little eyes and tried to remember what I was thinking when I was so still, but I had no clue so my mind wandered and before long I didn't remember about the string missing and I plucked the key out of my shirt pocket and popped it into my mouth. I stuck my tongue out so Seth Justman could see the key from his desk in the next row. 'What'll you give me if I swallow this?' I whispered.

'A dollar,' he said. And he was good for it too because he wasn't on free breakfast and free lunch, so I knew he had food money on him.

This will be easy money, I thought. So I worked up my mouth full of saliva and swallowed hard and the key scraped down my throat a little sideways. But I did it. All the way down! I opened my mouth to show Seth and he was pretty amazed and dug into his pocket and gave me a dollar. Then I reached for my chin to pull the string but I only felt my lips, and suddenly I remembered there was no string and I hopped straight up onto my seat screaming, 'Mrs Maxy, I ate my key!'

Everyone spun round and stared at me, and Mrs Maxy's eyes bugged out because she knew she had cut the string.

'Oh my Lord,' she shouted. She grabbed me and ran to Mrs Deebs's room next door. 'Watch my class,' she cried in a desperate voice, and then trotted me down to the nurse.

Nurse Holyfield listened calmly to Mrs Maxy, who was anything but calm. Then she unlocked a white cabinet and removed a small brown bottle and plastic spoon. 'Ipecac,' the nurse explained. 'It'll make you throw up like a champ, I promise.'

She gave me a green plastic dish to hold under my chin. It looked like a wading pool for Sea Monkeys. Then she gave me a spoonful of medicine that tasted so bad it made me vomit up everything that I had eaten all last week. She stirred through the vomit with a plastic fork. But no key. She gave me a second spoonful and I gave her all of last year's food. Still no key.

'Should we call the doctor?' asked Mrs Maxy.

'Nay,' said the nurse. 'At this point it's either cut him open or let nature take its course.'

'I vote for nature,' I said.

'And I have a class to get back to,' Mrs Maxy said. 'I'll tell Mrs Jarzab he's down here and she can take care of him.'

While we waited the nurse said she wanted to play a game with me.

'I'm good at card games,' I said. 'Grandma taught me how to play poker.'

'No,' she said. 'I want to ask you questions and I want you to answer them.'

'What?' I asked. I was still thinking about poker and how much I missed Grandma.

'Well, you just answered my first question,' she said. 'Do you lose a lot of things?'

It wasn't that I hated being asked a bunch of questions. I had nothing against questions. I just didn't like listening to them, because some questions take for ever to make sense. Sometimes waiting for a question to

44

finish is like watching someone draw an elephant starting with the tail first. As soon as you see the tail your mind wanders all over the place and you think of a million other animals that also have tails until you don't care about the elephant because it's only one thing when you've been thinking about a million others.

'Do you lose a lot of things?' she asked.

'Keys,' I said, and gave her a big smile. 'One day I lost my trousers. I took them off in the bathroom and forgot where I left them.'

'Do you like animals?'

'I *love* animals,' I replied. 'I want to get a dog.'

When Mrs Jarzab, the principal, arrived, Nurse Holyfield talked with her out in the hall. When they were finished, Mrs Jarzab told me to follow her.

'Joey, you need a little extra help,' she said as we walked down the main hallway. 'Think of it this way. Students who have trouble with math get extra math help. Or if they have trouble reading we give them reading help.'

'I can read fine,' I said.

'That's right,' she said, and patted my head. 'But you can't sit still very long and keep your mind on your work. So, we're going to give you some sitting help.'

We went down a set of stairs to the basement. 'Are we going to visit the janitor?' I asked.

'No,' she replied. 'This summer we put in a special-ed room to help out kids who need some extra help or attention.'

'I heard about it,' I said. 'Mrs Maxy said I was going to be sent there if I didn't settle down.'

'She was right,' Mrs Jarzab replied. Then she opened a door and we went into a big, bright yellow room that still smelled from fresh paint.

'Everyone is very friendly,' she said. 'So don't be afraid. You'll probably know some of the children.'

But it was hard not to be scared. There were a few kids from upstairs, but the room was mostly filled with the hurt kids, the slow kids, the kids who steered their wheelchairs with their chins, the spastic kids who walked and talked funny and were brought to school in their own special bus or in special cars from home. I always wondered where they went once they arrived. Now I knew. Plus there were a lot of women hovering around who turned out to be moms, helping the teacher with their kids. It was pretty surprising to me that they weren't at work because mine was always working. But I guess these moms had a whole job just taking care of their kids, which is why I didn't belong there, otherwise my mom couldn't work.

'Can I go back up to my class now?' I asked Mrs Jarzab.

'After a while,' she replied. 'First, I need to introduce you to Mrs Howard.'

I looked away, far away to a shiny corner of the room because even my grandma taught me that it wasn't polite to stare at crippled kids. Then I looked back and a few of them were looking at me, which was OK because I was normal. I waved to them and they waved in return, some better than others, and I felt a little more relaxed thinking they were nice.

'I only broke a few rules,' I said to the principal. 'There's nothing wrong with me but that.'

'I know,' she said. 'But we're going to help you learn not to break them.'

'I've already learned that,' I said. 'I'll never swallow another key again, I promise.'

'I'm sure you won't,' she replied.

Just then Mrs Howard walked over and smiled at me.

'This is the student I spoke to you about,' Mrs Jarzab said to her. Then she turned to me. 'Joey,' she said, 'I want you to listen to Mrs Howard and do everything she tells you to do. We're going to give you a little extra help with sitting still and staying on task.'

I felt like some kind of bad dog that had pooped all over the carpet, eaten the slippers, and attacked the mailman, and was now being sent to obedience school.

Mrs Howard led me by my hand to the tall metal chair in the corner of the room. 'This,' she said, 'is the Big Quiet Chair. I call it step number one. The first thing I want to find out is how long you can sit still.'

I climbed up into the giant chair and sat back and just stared at her. I must have looked pretty calm on the outside, like I was really normal and that this was all a big mistake, because she smiled at me and gave me a dopey picture book to read. But inside my body I felt like a big bottle of warm Coke when you drop it in the grocery store and it begins to fizz out the top like a bomb about to blow. Then she went back to help some kid who still had his bicycle helmet on and had fallen over. I flipped through the book so fast I couldn't tell you a thing about it except that it was made out of paper. Then I picked at my finger bandage until I had it unrolled. And then I started rocking back and forth, but the chair wouldn't rock. So I heaved myself from side to side. It still didn't move. I gripped the arms and jerked myself around and hung way out over the arms like some rodeo rider on a wild bull. But the chair didn't budge. When I looked down at the legs I saw it was bolted to the floor. Bolted, as if I was some kind of circus freak. So I rocked even harder, then took the heels of my shoes and kicked at the legs, and since it was metal it started clanging real loud like the heating pipes and that's when Mrs Howard came dashing back over. She put her hands on my knees and I slowed down for a moment, then she reached down and untied my laces.

She held my sneakers in her hand and said, 'I'll be right back.' She went into a closet and returned with a pair of those fuzzy bunny-rabbit slippers, the kind with the big buck-teeth on the toes and long ears you can trip over. She put them on my feet and said, 'OK, you can kick the chair all you want. And every time you come here, until you sit still and stop kicking, you'll have to wear these slippers.'

Over her shoulder some of the moms were looking at me and they had tired faces. Not tired and mad like I had screwed up somehow and they were upset. It was different. They were tired from being so sad and now they were sad some more because *I* was screwed up too and they felt bad for me like they felt for their own kids because they figured I wasn't ever going to get better. And it made me so mad to be stared at like some hopeless kid that I kicked away at the chair legs until my heels were so sore they were bruised and it hurt to kick. Then suddenly, it just seemed all the energy drained out of me and the yellow walls were so bright I closed my eyes and fell asleep.

Towards the end of the day Mrs Howard woke me up and said it was time for me to go back up to Mrs Maxy's class so I could get my homework assignment. I did, only I was still wearing those buck-toothed rabbit slippers, and when I shuffled into class rubbing my eyes Seth Justman pointed at me and started to snicker and the whole class cracked up and Mrs Maxy had to clap her hands to settle everyone down, then she led me to my seat. She gave me an 'I mean business' look and tapped on my tasks list. 'Remember, Joey,' she said right into my ear, 'stick to the rules and you won't get into trouble.'

Even though she was being nice I didn't know what to say and I put my head down on my desk. It felt so cool against my cheek and I wanted to sleep some more.

'And I think you owe the class an apology for being disruptive earlier,' she said.

'I'm sorry I swallowed my key,' I said a little too loudly without raising my head. 'Really. I'm sorry.' But I didn't feel sorry and I could feel myself just wanting to jump up and run, so I hooked my slippers around the front legs of the desk and tried hard to look at one solid thing, like the big jack-o'-lantern on the window, and get a two-handed grip on my desktop, because if I slipped and lost concentration and didn't pay attention to my highlighted tasks list Mrs Maxy might have no other choice but to give up on me for good and send me full-time down to special ed. And there would be nothing I could do about it, or my mom, or anyone, because I've been warned so many times there is a file on my bad behaviour as thick as the phone book. So I hung on to my desktop and with all my might I held myself in my seat as if some giant was holding me, and I don't think I even breathed until the bell rang and I blasted out of my seat and headed for home still wearing those dumb slippers.

I was sitting on the porch when Mom returned from work and I just mixed her a drink and didn't whisper a word about what happened today. But she found out anyway when Mrs Jarzab called the house later that night.

# 5.

# Make a Wish

Before bed, Mom had given me a couple of spoonfuls of laxative. The next morning nature took its course. I was sitting on the toilet with my new bedroom slippers on when I heard *splash-clunk* as the key fell out of my butt and hit the porcelain bowl. I put on my mom's rubber cleaning gloves, crammed some toilet paper up my nose, took a swampy breath through my mouth, and fished it out. It was nasty, but the key looked the same after I washed it off.

At school, I walked into class with my hands clasped together up over my head like the

World Wrestling Champion of the Universe. 'I pooped it out!' I shouted. 'I pooped it out in the toilet.'

Seth Justman cheered. 'Did you save it?' he asked.

What did he think? That I'd throw it away? I pulled it up from the new string around my neck. 'Same key,' I said. 'Wanna sniff?'

'Do it, do it, do it,' Seth shouted, and instantly the class shouted along with him. Mrs Maxy was busy down the hall with Mrs Deebs organizing our field trip. I was so excited I forgot to ask for money and I put the key in my mouth and swallowed.

'Aggh,' everyone groaned, but they loved it.

'Gross,' Seth shouted. 'You swallowed a turd-flavoured key.'

Then I slowly pulled it up as if there was a drum roll in the air. It was kind of hard coming because my throat was scraped up and when I got it all the way out I saw why. I had eaten a bowl of cold spaghetti for breakfast and the strands were dangling off the head of the key like tiny octopus legs. I bounced it up and down for everyone to see and they squealed so loud Mrs Maxy came flying in.

'I knew it would have to be you,' she said,

wagging her finger at me as she turned the corner and saw my catch. 'Now go down to the nurse and clean your face and mouth. And bring me back the key.'

Nurse Holyfield listened to what I had done and then gave me a little paper cup with some mouthwash that tasted like the stuff my mom drinks.

'I'd have made a million dollars,' she said, 'if I could figure out a way to put an on-off switch on guys like you.'

'Want to touch my key?' I asked, and held it up.

'Did you take your meds today?' she asked in return.

'Can I get back to you on that?' I sang.

'I think I already know the answer,' she said, giving me a disapproving look. 'You can't take them only when you feel like it,' she continued as she took me to the toilet to wash.

'I know that,' I sputtered. 'But Mom forgot.'

'We can give them to you here,' the nurse said. 'I have kids lining up every day for their meds.'

'No way,' I replied. 'Mom said no-one is ever to give me medicine but her.'

'Then make sure you take it,' she stressed. 'Do the right things for yourself.'

'I am,' I said. 'I'm washing my face.' When I looked up at her she was shaking her head.

'You better get back to class,' she said, and handed me a paper towel. 'You're a smart boy but you'll fall behind if you don't keep at your work.'

'How smart am I?' I asked.

'Smart enough to know how to press my buttons,' she said. 'Now scoot.'

Mrs Maxy had cleared a spot on her bulletin board and after I gave her the key she tacked it on the cork. 'Every morning your key goes up here,' she said. 'And every afternoon, you can pick it up. Now, do you know why I'm doing this?' she asked.

'Can I get back to you on that?' I said.

'OK, wise guy. That's enough smart talk for one day,' she said. 'Now go downstairs and see Mrs Howard for a focus session. If you calm down you can join your class after lunch for math.'

'See you later, alligators,' I said to the class. I grabbed my ruler and walked out of the room backwards like I was sword-fighting an entire army and I stayed walking backwards, stabbing and slapping the lockers all the way down to Mrs Howard's dungeon.

'I'm back,' I said when I pushed open the door with my butt.

Mrs Howard was setting frosted cupcakes on everyone's desks. 'Oh, how nice to see you, Joey,' she replied, and gave me a big smile. 'You're just in time for Harold's birthday party.'

'I love parties,' I said right back and waved to all the moms. They smiled at me and waved. I knew they would like me once they got to know me. Everyone did.

'Can I help?' I asked.

'Yes,' said Mrs Howard. She pointed to a stack of rainbow party hats. 'You can pass those out.'

The kids who could put on their own hats I left to themselves. But the ones who couldn't move so well I helped, until we all, even the moms and Mrs Howard and me, were wearing party hats, and we sang a very crazy 'Happy Birthday' to Harold, who was in a neck brace and couldn't blow out his own candle. Mrs Howard held the candle an inch from his mouth and he just jerked his head back and forth and kept spitting little bubbles. But the flame hung in there. And we were gathered around him in a circle, and everyone was pulling for him like the candle was a fuse on a bomb and we were all going to be blown to shreds if he didn't put it out. Harold kept trying, and still he had no wind in him, just those little bubbles. And the candle was getting shorter and shorter and whatever it was he wished for was not going to come true but just sputter out in the blue icing. I looked into his face as hard as I could and it was like I heard him screaming inside, 'Come on! Don't just stand there. Do something!' I looked around at the adults and they were all leaning forward, but were frozen as if they didn't know what to do next. But I did, which meant it was up to me. Everyone wanted the candle blown out so I stepped forward, took a big breath, and when I let it out I made Harold's wish come true and thought, Maybe now there is a pot of gold under that tilted rainbow hat.

Everyone gasped and looked at me as if I had just stabbed Harold. But I had done him a favour.

'I helped you get your wish,' I said to him. And he jerked his head around like a spastic robot and I could tell he was happy.

'See,' I said to everyone as I pointed at Harold's mouth. 'He's smiling, 'cause I helped him out.'

That's exactly when Mrs Howard took my hand and led me across the room. 'I think you need to settle down for a few minutes,' she said. She made me sit in the Big Quiet Chair and read a book that couldn't be read because when I looked at the letters they kept sliding off the page like drops of mercury when you smash open a thermometer, which is something I know about. I kept asking for a cupcake but Mrs Howard said, 'The last thing you need is sugar.' And she gave me a carrot.

'What's up, Doc?' I said to her, and chewed the carrot really loudly with my mouth open.

But she didn't answer because just then Mrs Jarzab opened the door and brought in a scary-looking new kid who she said had come to our class from a school that didn't have their own special room.

I never did make it back up to Mrs Maxy's class for math like I wanted to, and when school was over I walked home. That's when I found out I'd left my key on the bulletin board, so I just lay down flat on the porch to hide from the bad kids and waited again for my mom. I was thinking about her all afternoon because of something I wanted to ask her.

When she turned the corner I ran up to her and tugged on her arm. 'Can I ask you a question?'

'One minute,' she said, and gave me her bag to hold.

We went inside and she undressed, and hung her dirty work clothes that smelled like bleach on the back of the bedroom door, and put on her bathrobe, and all the time I kept saying, 'Can I ask now? Can I?'

'Just let me wind down for a moment while you tell me where your key is,' she said. I told her about the bulletin board as I followed her to the kitchen and watched as she fixed herself a drink. She sat down at the breakfast table and opened the newspaper and hid her face behind the huge pages as if she were reading the wings of a giant butterfly.

'Now?'

'Count to a hundred first,' she said.

I was counting the numbers off as if I was running down a huge flight of stairs, and staring at the colour photos of a car crash on the front of the newspaper.

'Now?' I asked, after I had counted to a hundred.

'OK,' she said. 'Fire away.'

'Did I eat paint chips when I was a baby?'

'No, just potato chips,' she said, and turned the page.

'Well, did I ever fall on my head?' I asked.

'Mostly your butt,' she said.

'Did you drink a lot when you were pregnant with me?'

She paused, and I could tell the fun was over. She didn't lower the paper, so I couldn't see her face.

'No more than the usual,' she finally said, as if she was far away, reading something.

'What's usual?' I asked. 'I don't know what's usual. You know. What?' And as I spoke I could feel my heart just picking up speed so I closed my eyes and sat on my hands because sometimes that helps settle me down like I'm in my own straitjacket.

'A glass of wine with dinner and an Amaretto sour after.' She said it like she had said it a million times already, and she was sick of saying it. And then she began to fight back. She lowered the pages for a moment. 'Why are you asking? *Why? Why?*'

She knew when she asked 'why' that the millions of little gears in my head just jammed all together. She knew I could never get to the *why* of anything. I could never get my mind to gather exactly what I wanted to say, and I could never find the trail to the bottom of what I meant. There were so many other trails that wandered off along the way, and me with them.

'We got a new kid today in specials,' I said as she rattled the paper, with my heart climbing high up into my chest. 'And I heard one of the moms say he is "over the fence and long gone" from his mom drinking too much when he was the size of a peanut. And he's skinny, and his head is so small, like a kicked-around softball and he can't do *nothing*, I mean *nothing*. Like my worst day is better than his best day. Ever.'

'Then count your blessings,' she said, turning the page. 'And don't go looking for ways to blame me for your problems. Other people drink wine and their kids are geniuses. You could've gone either way.'

I still couldn't see her face, but it was like I

could see her voice and it said, 'Don't push me. Just stop now and turn around before you go too far and get hurt.'

And so I buttoned my lip and just went back to eating the salty nuts out of the big bowl of party mix and then she lowered the paper and I saw two small wet spots where she held it across her lap. She was crying but I didn't know if it was because she drank too much or if it was just the everyday sadness of her life with me.

She sniffed and sniffed as if she were pulling something up hand over hand on a rope, as if to pull it all back into her eyes and nose, and then she said, 'Why me? Why? I try so hard.'

I don't have an answer to that one. But someday all that asking me 'why?' is going to wear my brain down so that it is as smooth as a boiled egg and I'll just sit in Mrs Howard's big chair all my life like the coma kids and that word *why* will float through me from ear to ear like a warm breeze. We have a kid in specials named Kerwin Klump and Mrs Howard calls him 'My cute little lump,' but not in any kind of mean way. And he doesn't do much but sit there and drool and then every now and again he jumps up and pulls the plastic fire alarm. He did it a couple of times to the real one in the hallway during the first week of school, so they put a fake fire alarm in the specials room and he can pull that without the whole school having to empty out and the fire trucks arriving with ambulances screaming right behind them. And all the while Kerwin hopping up and down like he's permanently on a pogo stick, saying, 'I bad. I bad.'

No, I'm not like Kerwin. I can have good days. Entire days when I wake up and I'm calm inside like water when it's not boiling, and I just plant my feet on the floor like every kid in America and do a sleepy walk down to the bathroom and take a nice hot shower and wash my hair and dry off and get dressed and eat breakfast and all the while thinking about what I'd like to do with my day. And then the most amazing thing to me is after I think about what I want to do, like read, or see a friend, or say something nice to Mrs Howard, or write a poem, I actually do all that stuff. That is *amazing* to me. I think it, then I do it. This may be how everyone else operates, but this is not how I usually operate. Usually I wake up with springs popping inside my head, like I'm in the middle of a pinball game where I'm the ball, and I shoot out of bed and directly to the kitchen where I ricochet around after food until by chance I snatch some toast, then go slamming off the padded stool tops like they were lighted bumpers and zing up the hall and into the bathroom where I try to brush my teeth, but I brush mostly my lips and chin and then I explode back out the door and across the living room and bounce off the furniture until Mom gets a grip on me and wipes the toothpaste off my face and works a pill down my throat. Then she holds the back of my head and pushes my face into her soft belly and just holds me like that for a few minutes, and if the meds are working I begin to settle down real well and when I pull my face away and look up at her she is smiling and stroking my head and if she is in a good mood we both start to laugh because it is so funny that I've just gone from being Ricochet Rabbit to Charlie Brown in no time flat. And this makes both of us so happy. I love it when she rescues me like this, and when the meds work, and when I go to school and stay in my seat and kids don't call me Zippy and teachers pat me on the head at the end of the day and give me gold and blue foil stars and say nice things to me, and later when Mom comes home I tell her how good I've been and she smiles and smiles and I get so pumped up I run to mix her an Amaretto sour and she keeps smiling and then calls me her genius, her hypersmart buddy, and we laugh.

# 6.

# who?

My day started out great. All the fourth- and fifth-grade classes got to go to a traditional Amish farm for a field trip. There must have been about a hundred of us because we filled two long orange buses. My morning meds were working and I had a window seat and just loved watching all the cars and houses and fields speeding by, and when Mrs Maxy was busy with other kids I sat up on my knees and stuck my head out the top window and felt the breeze sweep past me so fast and hard it made everything in my head stand still. That was the best part of my day right there, sticking my head out the window like a dog.

When we got off the bus Mrs Maxy and Mrs Deebs and two other teachers and a gang of moms had us all line up, and Mrs Maxy gave everyone the lecture about 'respecting differences in other cultures so no pointing and snickering or unpleasant comments, or you sit on the bus. You got that?' We did, or we didn't, but nobody knew which just yet. Once that was out of the way we marched toward the front steps of the farmhouse as if we were a line of ants dressed in clothes.

'Stop,' hollered Mrs Deebs when we reached the steps. When she said 'stop' she meant it because she had extra-short hair and a big head on a really wide body that there was no getting around. Every time her head moved left or right I thought it was about to roll down her sloping shoulders like a boulder down a hill.

Two clean-looking Amish girls in long blue dresses and starched white aprons came out and said, 'Welcome. The Amish have been in Lancaster County since the seventeen hundreds. We are a people who keep alive the traditions of the past. Please follow us inside to see our plain and simple way of life, our crafts and cooking.'

For a moment I thought how it would have been so funny if kids took a field trip to my house when me and my grandma were living together. We'd step out the front door and say, 'Welcome. Our place looks like a tornado's just hit. Run around inside like we do and have a blast!'

The Amish girls led us across the porch, which had a line of rocking chairs, so while I was waiting my turn to get inside I ran from chair to chair giving each one a good push as if a family of ghosts was rocking, until one of the moms gave me a look and pointed to the end of the line which meant I had already lost my place.

Finally, I stepped through the front door. In the large room to one side were a bunch of old ladies with handkerchief hats on their heads. They were huddled together like a circle of mushrooms after a rainstorm and hand-sewing a big quilt with huge sunflower stars in the middle. In the next room more ladies were hooking rugs and doing needle-point, and even though the moms were all oohing and ahhing as if they were watching fireworks I started not to listen to any of it because I smelled something really good and sweet coming from down the hall and after just one whiff of that smell I couldn't pay close attention to anything else. We passed a few more rooms and I didn't care if the Amish were doing card tricks or shaving their beards off. My eyes were watered over and that smell had me staggering like a zombie.

After a lot of polite and very boring questions and answers about Amish life one of the Amish girls led us the rest of the way down the hall into a huge kitchen. By then the sweet smell was so powerful I felt my nose swelling up, just getting bigger and bigger, and I had to touch it with both hands to make sure it wasn't growing like Pinocchio's. It was still the same old size, but that smell was so overwhelming to me I couldn't get enough of it and I just kept gulping down huge breaths as if I could eat the air.

'Every product made in this typical Amish kitchen is based on what nature provides,' one of the girls said. 'We make butter and cheese. Bread and biscuits, jam and jellies. But we are especially famous for our molasses shoofly pie.'

At first I didn't think I heard her right. 'A pie made out of shoes and flies and molasses?' I said to Seth.

'I bet it's really good,' he said. 'You should ask for some with extra flies.'

'Yeah,' I said, and was thinking about the pie so much I didn't hear another word the girl said about Amish cooking secrets. The thought of a pie made out of shoes and flies was amazing me. And really, I didn't care if they made their pies out of sweaty socks and wiggle worms, as long as they turned out this sweet-smelling I'd eat them. Even as I stood there the sweetness was making me dizzy. I experimented and closed my eyes and took a deep breath, and I had to open my eyes quickly as I stumbled into Seth and he gave me a shove back and called me a moron. By the time I pulled myself together Mrs Deebs was saying, 'OK, everyone line up for a little piece of shoofly pie before we go to the garden, and later to the barn.'

All I could think about was shoes and flies as I stood in line, and from where I was at the back I didn't see any kids spit it out, so it must have been good. I dropped down on my knees to see what kind of shoes the Amish girls were wearing. They may have had some special shoe tradition I didn't know about. Maybe their shoes were made out of liquorice or rock candy. But their dresses were so long I couldn't see their shoes and a mom gave me a stern look and yanked me up by the back of my shirt, as if I was trying to peek up their dresses.

'Mind your manners, young man,' the mom said with her eyebrows raised.

'I'm just doing research,' I shot back.

When it was close to my turn Mrs Maxy called me to one side and whispered, 'That pie is not good for you, Joey. It's got too much sugar. So it's better to just stick to fruit.'

She must have seen the hurt look on my face because I couldn't hide it. It felt like my whole face turned into a crumpled piece of paper. And then she reached forward and handed me a small white napkin with an apple slice on it that had already turned brown on the edges.

'It has cinnamon on it,' she said. 'It's very good.'

'I don't want this,' I replied. 'I want the shoe fly pie.'

'Don't make an issue out of it,' she said

firmly. 'We're just doing what is best for you.'

And she didn't want to talk about it any more because other kids were beginning to bunch up at the back door and stare at us.

'Now move along,' she said to the kids. 'If you've already had your pie, go over to the pumpkin patch and carve—'

And then she stopped talking, like she was saying something wrong in front of me, as if she wanted to spell it out like adults do when they want to keep a secret from kids who can't spell. I took the apple slice and put it in my back pocket and kept on wondering why she didn't finish telling me about the carving.

It didn't take long to find out. A few minutes later we were all in the pumpkin patch with our baby pumpkins that we were allowed to pick off the vines. The Amish girls were handing out wood-handled carving tools and all the kids were sitting at picnic tables surrounded by the moms who were helping them.

I ran up to the Amish girl and got my tool, but Mrs Maxy was right on me.

'Joey, you can't have that knife,' she said. 'It's dangerous.'

I looked at the knife. The blade was real stubby and about an inch long and it wasn't even that sharp. It was more like safety scissors.

'It's not dangerous,' I said. 'Besides, my mom lets me slice bread and stuff.'

'We just don't want you to hurt yourself,' she said calmly.

'I want to carve one too,' I said.

'You can draw on one now,' she suggested, and held out a black marker. 'And we'll carve it later. I promise.'

'I want to do it now with everyone else,' I said, and held the knife behind my back.

'Later,' Mrs Maxy said. 'All the moms are busy helping other kids.'

'Now!' I shouted, and my fists balled up and I could feel that surge of energy run through me like nothing in the world was going to keep me from doing what I wanted.

'Give me the knife,' she ordered, and held out her hand.

'No,' I said, and stepped back, then threw it as far as I could into the pumpkin patch.

'I think it's time for you to go have a time-out in the bus,' she said, getting tired of me. 'If you can sit still for ten minutes and calm down, you can come back here and draw on your pumpkin.'

'Everyone else gets to carve theirs,' I said, pointing to all the other kids who were busy scratching out big evil eyes and teeth with their unsharp baby knives.

'We just don't want any more accidents,' she said, and pointed towards the bus in front of the house. 'Now be a good boy and go directly to the bus. I'll be watching from here, and when we get ready to tour the barn I'll get you.'

I turned around and stomped back alongside the farmhouse, and for a moment I thought I'd just keep walking all the way home and get my own knife and carve my own pumpkin. But I felt Mrs Maxy's eyes staring at the back of my head so I didn't. And then I passed a window and smelled that sweet pie again. I glanced back over my shoulder and some kid was pulling on her sleeve and talking to her, so instead of walking home or going to the bus I sneaked round to the front door of the farmhouse. The quilt ladies were still working as I marched by quickly down to the kitchen. The Amish girls were out in the garden and no-one else was on guard so I grabbed a whole shoe fly pie off the table because it popped into my head to do it and by then my feet were moving a mile a minute and I opened a side door and headed out beyond the barn toward the cornfield. I ducked down low and ran between two rows of tall stalks until I couldn't see anything around me but corn plants. I sat down and stuck my finger straight through the brown crust as if it were a knife and I carved out a broken-looking Halloween face on the pie, and when I was finished I stuck my finger in my mouth.

It was sweet, as sweet as the little packets of sugar I eat at Dunkin' Donuts, sweeter maybe. More like pancake syrup right out of the bottle the way I drink it if Mom even for a second lets it stay out on the counter. And the pie was almost as runny as the syrup. It wasn't gelled up like the cafeteria cherry pie. So I picked the top crust off and ate that first while I stirred my finger around trying to find the shoes and flies. But it was just all molasses, so I felt tricked but didn't know how. Then I just kept sticking my two curled fingers in and licking them off and the more I ate the faster I wanted to eat it and nothing else mattered. Not the real flies sticking to my fingers and lips, not the wind blowing through the cornstalks, not the voices overhead of kids carving pumpkins. Nothing. Just eating the pie and tasting the warm sugar melt all over my tongue and ooze down into my belly like a slippery sugary snake, and when it was almost finished I bent the tin pie plate in half, tilted back my head, and poured the last brown drops of it right down into my throat. Then I licked the plate like a dog, and by the time I finished my mind was a mess and my legs were pumping. I was ready to run a circle round the entire world.

I had a funny sound in my head, kind of a hissing like when the TV station goes off the air at night and there is nothing but static, but really loud static and no words at all and getting louder like tyres speeding down a wet road and coming right at me. My eyes felt so swollen with the flood of energy inside my throbbing head that I could only see the tops of my cheeks and a smudge where my nose fitted on and a bigger blur beyond that. I took a deep breath and the air gushed into my lungs and lifted me up and suddenly I was running and crashing through the stalks of the cornfield. I had my arms stuck out like the wings of a plane, and the long curved leaves sliced me up but I didn't feel the stinging. I didn't feel my feet hit the ground, I didn't feel the jolt when I tripped forward and slammed into the cornstalks and clods of dirt with my chest and bounced right up and kept going. I was running so fast and breathing so deep that I thought I could take off up out of the cornfield and higher into the blue air and above into the clouds and look down on the farm and bus and the kids and Mrs Maxy, who would be pointing up at me.

Then before I could slow down I was suddenly running out of the cornfield and from there I headed for the barn where there was a huge open door so I went inside and I was not saying to myself, 'See the ladder. Climb the ladder.' No, I was just climbing before I knew it and I was up way high on the big timbers playing a crazy kind of snakes and ladders, sliding down the tilted beams and climbing others like a monkey on a coconut tree. My spring was wound so tight that I was more like a rat in a maze, without words, or any feelings, or any ideas about myself and what I should be doing other than *go, go, go, up, up, up,* faster and higher until there was nothing more above me but the roof and an owl, one of those big white owls with the huge dark eyes and hooked beak, which is where I stopped.

'Who?' it said. 'Who?'

And I answered, 'Joey Pigza. That's who.'

'Who?' it said again, and kept its eyes right on my face, and for some reason it was the same as if someone had asked me *why* I ate the pie, and *why* I was all the way at the inside top of the barn. And before I knew it my gears started shifting and all the energy inside me went somewhere else. I sat as still as a bookend with my chin on my knees and looked down from the rafter, and the ground was way beneath me with a hundred really small fourth- and fifth-graders pointing up into the air and one of them was calling my name. It was Mrs Maxy.

'Joey,' she hollered, and waved her hands over her head like she was in trouble. 'Joey, don't move. We're coming to get you.'

And in a few minutes the biggest ladder I ever saw was being raised up from the back of a horse and wagon and an old man with a long white beard wearing a big black hat was climbing up as if he was Santa for the Amish.

'Don't worry, son,' he said. 'Just stay put. That owl don't bite.'

'Me either,' I said, squeezing some words out of my brain. I stood up on both feet and began to walk the big beam and everyone below looked so tiny and they were all yelling for me to sit down. But I didn't want to sit. It was the last thing in the world I wanted to do. I just kept walking across the huge room until below me was a pile of hay bales. And I had seen about a million movies of kids falling in hay and bouncing up and down and running off, so it seemed no different than playing stuntman or jumping into piles of fallen leaves so I yelled out, 'Ger-on-i-mo!' as I jumped.

The best part was being in the air, sort of wiggling as if I was doing a hula dance to keep from landing on my head, and then I hit the hay with my feet first and it wasn't soft like the movies but so hard that it felt like something had landed on me instead of me landing on it. I didn't even sink into it like leaves or anything. It was more like landing on a huge pin-cushion and each time I bounced down on it I was jabbed a hundred more times. But none of it hurt as much as my ankle when I tried to stand up. I must have twisted it, and instead of being able to run away I tried to crawl, but by then another old farmer was on me. 'I got him,' he hollered to those who were still to come.

'Joey,' Mrs Maxy said when she came running over, 'what got into you?' And then she must have seen all the molasses on my face and shirt and she put two and two together. Her face first got mad but then when the farmer put me down on my feet and I fell over to one side because of the pain in my ankle she got all worried again.

'Let's see that ankle,' she said, and untied my shoe with her nervous hands, which hurt because my ankle was a little swollen and looked more yellow than it should have.

'Oh, Joey.' She sighed, and tried to feel for broken bones. 'What are we going to do here?'

'I didn't mean to get hurt,' I said. 'I just wanted to jump in the hay.'

'I know,' she said. 'It's just that there is always a difference between what you think you are doing and what happens to you and everyone else.'

I looked up and there was Maria

Dombrowski writing my name down on a pad because Mrs Maxy had told her to keep a list of everyone who 'got out of line'. And everyone else, teachers and parents and Amish, were all looking at me as if they were at the zoo and I was something in a cage.

'I'll be OK,' I said, and pulled my foot out of her hands and stood up. 'But my shoe doesn't fit any more so they can have it for their pie.' I pointed at the Amish girls and they began to giggle and cover their mouths. Then everyone began to laugh. Except for Mrs Maxy. I don't think she got the joke.

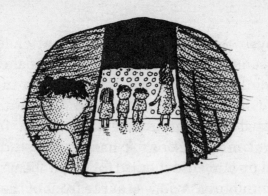

# 7.

# Gifted and Talented

Mrs Maxy had a conference in the morning so our class had a substitute named Miss Adams, who didn't know me from Adam. This was a good break because after the field trip Mrs Maxy said she and me and Mrs Howard and Mrs Jarzab and my mom and Nurse Holyfield were all going to have a big meeting to discuss the 'next step' for me. I knew she wasn't talking about my ankle. That much I was sure of.

But since Mrs Maxy didn't show up I stopped worrying about what might happen. There were other things going on right before my eyes. After Miss Adams took attendance it was announced over the loudspeaker in the classroom that all the students in the gifted and talented programme were to be released to meet in the auditorium for a special presentation. A handful of students stood up and I did too and followed them right out the door. Maria was at the front of the line and I was the last, so she didn't even see me or she'd have snitched.

I knew if Mrs Jarzab saw me she would be upset about yesterday and probably send me down to Mrs Howard, so instead of going in the regular auditorium door I went around to the side door that opened to the back of the stage. I had gone in there before because when the huge velvet stage curtain was pulled open I loved to hide between the folds on one end, and I could stand there for ever wrapped up in the soft blue velvet like a caterpillar in a cocoon.

So I tiptoed onto the back of the stage and slipped into one of the folds of the curtain and stood still with the dusty velvet tickling my nose.

Before long Mrs Jarzab introduced a woman named Mrs Cole who had written a book on 'character counts', which was one of Mrs Jarzab's favourite slogans. Then she introduced Mrs Cole to the gifted and talented students and said they were a very special bunch of children. 'The cream of the crop,' she called them.

Mrs Cole was very excited and began to speak as loud and intense as a television preacher. 'Special people have to do special things for others less fortunate,' she declared. 'This is one of the great duties for people of exceptional *character*.'

In a roundabout way she was talking to me. I knew I'd never be part of the gifted and talented kids. That much was true. But I was one of the *special* people. My mom said I was special, the nurse said I was special, and I was also in special ed. So I really listened to everything she had to say, and I liked what I heard, that because we were the special kids we had to make sure we put our energy and talent to work for the benefit of the whole world. 'Think of it this way,' she said as if she were telling the greatest secret ever. 'All of you in the room have the power to change the world for the better. You might invent something like computers. Discover a cure for AIDS and save millions of lives. Like Mother Teresa, you might devote yourself to helping people who have no-one else to help them. Perhaps you could be the president and set an example of superior leadership. Or you could contribute your time and effort to build a better community.'

She went on and on about how it was up to the special gifted and talented kids to lead the way for others and that if we each pledge to be a positive force in the world then the world will be a better place for everyone. 'And it all starts one person at a time,' she said. 'So I want each of you today to accomplish something special that is an example to your peers that *character counts.*'

Everyone clapped, but I didn't dare so I did a sneaky clapping by blinking my eyes up and down real fast. What she said was true. Already I was thinking about something I could do during the day that would make the world a better place because of me, Joey Pigza.

After the assembly I didn't want to go back to class so I hobbled down to the nurse to have her check on my ankle. From all that standing it started to throb. I knew nothing big was wrong with it, but the throbbiness gave me a reason to see the nurse, who was always happy to see me.

I was wearing an ordinary shoe on one foot and I had the rabbit slipper from Mrs Howard on the one that was twisted. The nurse looked at my ankle, then squeezed it, and flipped it back and forth. 'This is nothing,' she said, and nicked my chin with her fist. 'Swallowing the key was worse.'

'I could never swallow my ankle,' I said as a joke.

'Lord, I hope not,' she said, and laughed. 'I don't think nature would take its course.' Then she took a bandage out of a metal cabinet and wrapped the ankle up for me tight so that it felt better. 'You can keep the bandage,' she said. 'As long as you use it.'

'OK,' I said. 'I was thinking of using it to wrap myself up like a mummy for Halloween. Do you have any more?'

'I have some old ones,' she said. 'But first, let's get your ankle healed before we mummify you. OK?'

'OK,' I agreed. I loved being agreeable. I loved the nurse and I thought she did a lot of special things so I told her in a whisper I snuck in to the gifted and talented speech. 'And Mrs Cole told us to do one really good thing today,' I said to her.

'I think that is an excellent idea,' Mrs Holyfield whispered back. 'So what do you have in mind?'

'I'm still thinking about it,' I said. 'But it's coming.'

'Well, keep working at it,' she said.

'I am,' I replied, and stood up. As long as I walked in straight lines and didn't twist my foot right or left then it didn't hurt so much.

'See you later,' she said.

After lunch I returned to the classroom instead of going out to break. I wanted to work on my new idea to change the world even though I could feel my meds wearing down like they do every time I eat something.

Mrs Maxy was back and sitting at her desk filling out some papers.

'Hi,' I said. 'Did you have a nice morning?'

'Yes, I did,' she replied, then asked, 'How's your ankle?'

'Better. Did you notice anything extra in your desk drawer?' I asked.

'I did,' she said.

I lifted my chin and smiled right back at her.

'It seems some secret admirer of mine left me a slice of cinnamon apple in my drawer.'

'Can you guess who that nice kid might be?'

'I bet it's the kid who's going to have the best behaviour all afternoon,' she said.

'I bet it is too,' I replied.

'You know we still have to have that talk,' she said, still smiling. 'You really lost it yesterday.'

'Yeah, but I've changed already. I sneaked out and went to the gifted and talented assembly and now I'm ready to do something great for the whole world.'

'Sneaking out doesn't lead me to believe that you've changed at all,' she replied.

'Yeah, but I only broke a little rule,' I replied. 'And now I can do something great for the world.'

'Really?' she asked. 'What do you have in mind?'

'I'm going to make a million bumper stickers for cars that say "Hate Is Not a Family Value". My mom saw one at work and said she wished she had a million of them to put on every car in the world.'

'*That* is very thoughtful,' she said. 'But I

don't think you should stick things on people's cars.'

'I won't,' I said. 'Mom will. I better get going. I only have a few minutes before everyone comes back from break.'

'Well, go to the back of the room and use the art supplies,' she said. 'If you stay on task I'm sure you can get a million done on time.'

So I went to the back of the room and got a thick piece of poster board. I took my time and drew wide lines across it and between each line I printed out the bumper-sticker saying in big block letters. I took a Day-Glo marker and outlined the word HATE to grab everyone's attention. When I finished I held the big poster up and over my head. 'Mrs Maxy, look,' I shouted.

She lifted her head from her work and gave me the thumbs up. Then she gave me a little secret wink and a smile because even though I'm difficult I'm very special and smart. Everyone says so.

'Very good printing,' she said. 'Nicely done, Joey.'

*Nicely done, Joey*, echoed in my mind over and over. I loved how that sounded and I didn't want to have any other words come into my head again. Ever. Just those three, *Nicely done, Joey*.

But suddenly I remembered I had to finish up fast. I got the safety scissors and began to cut the poster board into bumper-sticker-sized strips. But the poster board was too thick and the scissors kept twisting over onto their side and the harder I squeezed the more my fingers hurt.

Then the bell rang and kids started to pile in from the playground. I wanted to finish cutting my bumper stickers, so when Mrs Maxy got up from her desk to go stand in the hall and make sure nobody was running, I snuck up to her desk and opened the top drawer and grabbed her secret extra-sharp teacher scissors.

I was racing back to the bumper stickers with the scissors in my hand when it happened. I tripped over the stupid ear of the rabbit slipper and I sort of dived through the air with the open scissors stretched all the way out in front of me like some evil Big Bird's beak when Maria Dombrowski walked sideways across my path like a safety patrol guard and said, 'Slow down.' But I didn't and my hand collided with the side of her face and I went tumbling down the aisle.

I thought I was the one who was screaming because it was so loud I figured it had to be coming out of my mouth. But it wasn't me. I jumped up and didn't know what had happened at first, when, Oh my God, you should have seen the blood. It was like a pipe had burst. Blood just poured on to the floor from the cut end of her nose and she stood there shaking with her eyes wide open like she had stuck her finger in the electric socket. I bent over and picked up the tip of her nose, which now looked like the tiny end piece of a sliced banana. Then I stood up and pressed it back in place but the blood sprayed out in a circle like a shower nozzle. Oh, it was awful. Her mouth was wide open and no more sounds came out and I looked into her eyes and there was so much fear trapped in them I went instantly out of my mind, worse than Maria even. Worse than Mrs Maxy when a kid ran to tell her and she came flying into the room. And I was shrieking, 'I'm sorry! I'm sorry!' as I tried to pat her, pat the little nose piece back into place like it would stick and the blood would stop, and the cut would vanish, and I would run all the way to my poster which was going to change the world for the better.

Mrs Maxy yanked me away from Maria and I went spinning around like a top, screeching and hopping from desk to desk yelling, 'Sorry! Sorry!' Then I tried to wrestle the scissors from Mrs Maxy who had taken them from me because I wanted to cut my whole nose off to show just how sorry I was and give it to Maria, but Mrs Maxy wouldn't let me have the scissors and she kept shouting, 'Time out! Time out! Go to your corner.' But I was so nuts I couldn't tell you the difference between a corner and a circle or a square. And before long Nurse Holyfield arrived with a mile of gauze and white tape and began to bandage the nose with ice and, oh, I was like on fire just skipping around and then I heard the ambulance and then the principal came and threw her jacket over Maria's shoulders and they raced her out of the room. Believe me, it was bad, and everyone was staring at me like I was a maniac killer. I didn't know what else to do so I sat at my desk and ripped the ears off that rabbit slipper and stuffed them in my pockets and waited for something horrible to happen and it did.

Mrs Maxy was trying to clean up the mess and calm the class down when Mrs Jarzab returned with blood on her jacket and pointed at me.

'Joey,' she said from the front of the room. 'Bring your things and come with me.'

I pulled the front of my T-shirt way out and piled everything from inside my desk on it and carried it away. 'I'll be back,' I said over my shoulder to everyone because everyone was still staring at me and looking scared. 'I will.' And I was crying as I walked away and I couldn't see with the tears in my eyes and my stupid ankle hurt and I hit the edge of the door with my shoulder and it gave me cramp. I let go of one side of my T-shirt and my stuff fell all over the floor. I turned to look at Mrs Maxy and she was just biting her lip and I thought I could tell she really wanted me to stay. She knew I didn't mean to hurt anyone. Our eyes met and I said, 'I'm a good kid. I just got dud meds.' She winced, then turned her eyes towards the class and said, 'Now I want everyone to settle down. Take a deep breath, let it out slowly, and prepare to do some math.'

'Math is one of my strengths!' I shouted.

But by then Mrs Jarzab had picked up all my stuff and grabbed my hand like it too was a piece of my stuff and led me down the hall toward the office.

# 8.

# SUSPENDED

'It's one thing for him to hurt himself,' Mrs Jarzab said to my mother, pushing a flowered box of Kleenex toward her. Mom plucked a few out. She had changed the colour of her fingernails and they were so bright red her fingertips looked like mine when they were covered with wet blood while I was trying to fix Maria's nose.

We were sitting in the principal's office. I had been there since Mrs Jarzab pulled me out of class. My mom had been called in from the beauty parlour and was still wearing the white smock with her name, FRAN, embroidered on the front. She borrowed a car and got here so fast Maria had just left in the ambulance and Mom was still breathing heavily as she wiped away the lines of sweat around her neck.

'I'm sure it was just an accident,' my mother replied, and set the wad of damp Kleenex on the edge of the desk. 'Kids will be kids. Things like this happen.'

Mrs Jarzab pulled a Kleenex out of the box and used it to pick up Mom's like she was picking up something filthy. Then she tossed it in the trash can. 'There are special circumstances in this case,' Mrs Jarzab insisted, and tapped the top of my file. 'Joey has a history of being harmful to himself, and to others.'

'I know his history,' Mom said. 'I'm his mother. Nobody knows him better than me and even though there have been some problems in the past they are all accidental. Joey is not a mean child.' She was sweating down the side of her face as if *she* was in trouble for what had happened to Maria.

'I don't disagree that it was an accident,' Mrs Jarzab replied. 'What alarms me is the number of accidents that Joey is responsible for.' She opened my file. 'Let me cite what all happened this school year alone . . .'

'Just skip it,' my mother said, sounding a little angry like when people at work tick her off.

'Well, keep in mind we have informed you of his behaviour in the past . . .'

I started to ask Mom if she had any meds but she patted me on the leg. 'Let's just listen for now,' she whispered.

'. . . and the last time I warned you,' Mrs Jarzab continued, 'that if we didn't have the resources to help Joey here, that we would have to consider intensive counselling at the special-ed centre downtown, where he would receive the attention he needs.'

'I'm aware of all of this,' Mom said. But it was news to me.

'What special-ed centre?' I said suddenly. 'What—'

'Honey,' Mom interrupted. 'Just listen for a minute, while I do the talking.'

Mrs Jarzab had already put the Kleenex away and Mom reached for her own bag. When she unsnapped it I could smell the make-up and lipstick and perfume, especially the perfume, and I wanted to leap onto her lap and bury my head against her neck where she always put a dab of something extra nice and when I smelled it I just imagined following it to a safe, soft, warm Mom place that would protect me from everything bad and I could protect her.

'Joey,' Mom said. 'Joey.' She gave me a quick little pinch on my thigh and I snapped out of it.

'Yeah?' I said, real sleepy like I just woke up and wanted to go back to sleep. 'What?'

'Mrs Jarzab wants you to tell your side of the story.'

'What story?' I asked, kind of desperate, because I suddenly realized that they had been talking for a while and I had no idea what they'd been saying.

'Tell her,' Mom said, gently this time because she knew I had drifted far away. 'About the scissors.'

'Yes, tell me, Joey,' Mrs Jarzab said, with her face all nice and soft like there was nothing in the world she wanted to hear about but me and the scissors.

So I told her. 'I was making bumper stickers for me and my mom to change the world. And my safety scissors were too small for the paper so I got Mrs Maxy's out of her teacher drawer and was running when Maria jumped in front of me just when I tripped over my slipper ear. I fell forward and after I got up everyone said I cut off her nose tip.'

When I finished Mom was looking into her lap, and Mrs Jarzab was writing furiously on a pad. Then she stopped writing and looked up.

'Keep him at home tomorrow. The district special-ed bus will pick him up the day after. We need a day for the paperwork to go through.'

'OK,' Mom said. 'But this is temporary, right?'

'Because he has injured another student he has to be suspended for six weeks and receive mandatory counselling. That is school policy. But given Joey's record, he was bound to end up at the centre anyway, so maybe this is a blessing in disguise. What happens now is all up to him.'

We left the office and nothing more was said. All the way out to the car I kept staring at the ground to see if I could spot Maria's blood drops, or maybe she lost the tip of her nose and I thought if I could find it she would forgive me and I wouldn't be in so much trouble. For one second I thought I saw it and I reached down and snatched up a little flesh-coloured round thing, but it was just a used round Band-Aid. My mother slapped it out of my hand and that was the first moment I realized she was mad at me too. And suddenly it was as if my heart was as uncontrollable as my legs. All this time I thought she was on my side, because I was on her side. But maybe she had given up on me too. So I didn't say anything more because I was scared she was going to be against me like everyone else.

We drove away in silence. Not until we entered the Burger King drive-through did Mom speak again. She ordered for both of us without asking me what I wanted. And when we got the food from the side window Mom just pulled around the corner and parked on the street under a shady tree.

'I want to talk to you,' she said as she handed out the food. 'I've done my best,' she said. 'Do you understand that?'

'Yeah,' I replied. 'I know it's all me. I'm the one that's messed up, not you.'

I started eating my French fries. First the bottom end, then the top. I put the middle to one side. The middles didn't crunch when I bit into them so I saved them for last like a vegetable.

'You're not stupid, and you're not messed up,' Mom said. 'Don't think that.'

'Everybody else does,' I said, not looking at her face. 'Or they call me Retard. So really, messed up is nicer than Retard, or Brain-damaged, or Zippy the Pinhead.'

She just held a wad of napkins up to her eyes and her shoulders hunched forward and I knew she was crying because I had seen her trying to hide it from me a million times before.

'I pulled it together for you,' she finally said, and wiped her nose. 'When you were a baby I screwed up and left you behind but I loved you so much I pulled it together and came back to you. Now you have to pull it together for me,' she said. 'It's your turn. You owe me that much. You owe yourself, because if you don't pull it together now, I don't know what will happen next. But it is bound to be worse. Way worse than anything that has ever happened to you.'

I knew she was right. 'I'll have to go to a scary special-ed school,' I finally said, already crying by the time my face sunk into her shoulder.

'Just for a while,' she said, and rubbed my neck. 'Soon they'll see what a good guy you are and send you back.'

# 9.

# Bad seed

The next day I broke one of Mom's big rules. I left the house while she was at work and limped about ten blocks over to Maria's house. All the way over I practised what I wanted to say to her about how sorry I was, and I went over it again just before I knocked on her door.

It opened really fast and a big man in a mechanic's greasy jumpsuit who I figured must be her dad said, 'Who are you?'

'I'm Joey Pigza,' I replied, and I was very nervous because all the way over in my mind she was going to answer the door. I was ready for that. But it didn't turn out that way. Now I felt that I didn't know what to do, so I just said what I meant to tell her. 'I'm here to say I'm sorry,' I said, and I smiled like I had just stepped on the toe of a three-hundred-pound gorilla.

He pulled the door behind him to close off the house like I was going to trick him and run through his legs and attack Maria's nose again. 'Get out of here,' he said.

I held my two 'scissors cuts paper' fingers up in front of my face. 'I didn't come here with any scissors,' I said.

Then he stepped toward me. 'They shouldn't let messed-up kids go to school with normal kids,' he said.

I backed away. 'I'm only a little messed up,' I said quickly.

He stepped toward me again, quickly, as if he were going to pick me up like a chunk of log and heave me off the property. 'Come here,' he said, and reached for me.

Even with my bad ankle I was pretty quick and I turned and ran down the sidewalk. I glanced over my shoulder and he wasn't running at me but he was walking real quick like he just wanted to stick out his belly and bump me along. Behind him, in the big front window, Maria was watching with a huge bandage around her face and lots of silver 'Get Well' balloons floating above her head and a fluffy white puppy squirming in her arms. For a moment I didn't know what to do. I wanted to run over and apologize to her hurt face, and I wanted to run from him. But I just got jammed up, and as he came at me I stood there frozen and closed my eyes.

But he didn't hit me. 'Get out of here,' he said.

'It was an accident,' I replied. 'I'm not a bad kid.'

'I don't care if you are the Baby Jesus,' he said. 'You hurt my girl again and it'll be lights out for you and your whole family.'

'My mom had nothing to do with this,' I said.

He just looked at me with a nasty face, threw his head back and laughed. 'Your mom had *everything* to do with this.'

'That's a lie,' I said. 'She wasn't even there.' By then I was so mad at him for talking bad about my mom I was no longer afraid. 'My mom is not the problem,' I shot back at him. 'I am.' And I surprised him with that because he didn't know what to do next.

But I did. I put my hands on my hips, turned and walked off with my chin held high. And it wasn't until I went all the way back home and sat on the porch and remembered that I'd no longer be going back to my usual school that I got scared. I'd be somewhere else, with a lot of strange kids and teachers, and I have to tell you that all of this worried me so much I went inside the house and tried to find my meds because I wanted to take a bunch of them and return myself to normal.

But it was also one of Mom's rules to bring them to work with her. And she didn't break her own rules. So I just crawled up into the big comfy armchair and stared at the photograph of me being very still and gave myself a time-out. When Mom called to check up on me I told her everything was OK now.

That night, after Mom cooked a dinner of macaroni and cheese, we took a walk.

'I've been thinking about you all day,' she said, and kept her arm rested across my shoulders so that her warm hand covered my ear, which was nice because the wind was blowing.

'I've been thinking about you too,' I said,

looking up at her, then down at the sidewalk, then up at her again then down again because once I stepped on dog poop and slipped and never forgot it.

'Well, you've been on my mind because I have to work early tomorrow and can't see you on to the bus in the morning.'

'Oh,' I said in a small voice, and I felt my whole body get sad. 'I was hoping you could.'

'Me too,' she said softly, 'but I just couldn't shift my early appointments around at work. Those ladies get pretty fussy about having their hair done on time. Still, I have two presents for you.'

I looked up at her. 'Two?' I said. 'For me?' I love presents.

'The first one,' she said, 'doesn't look like a present. It isn't gift-wrapped. It doesn't have a ribbon around it, but I think it is a *huge* present.'

'Well?'

We stopped walking and stood still and she stared down at me and cupped my chin in her hand. 'My first present,' she said very seriously, 'is good advice. I want you to remember something that has always helped me. Whenever you think of something bad, you have to quickly think of something good. And you can never, never think of three things bad in a row or else you will just feel awful.'

'OK,' I said, wishing there was more to the present than advice. Something more I could hold in my hands.

'I mean it,' she said, because she knew I wasn't listening as seriously as she was talking.

'Does that mean if I have a good thought, then I have to think of something bad?' I asked, turning it all around.

'No,' she replied. 'You can think of all the good thoughts in a row you want.'

'OK, now what's my second present?' I asked, because the thrill of the first one had worn off quickly.

'It is a very *small* present,' she said.

'*Smaller* than the last one?' I shouted, and began to stagger as if I was wounded in action.

'Be patient. It starts small and gets bigger.'

We passed the ice cream parlour, where I knew I was never allowed to go. And the Polish-American club, where my grandmother said my dad spent some of his time 'bouncing around' before he went to Pittsburgh. And then we turned and walked into the second-hand book store.

'A book?' I asked, thinking that my presents were getting really small.

'A book is only part of it,' she said, and the way she was smiling told me it was really good. We walked to the back of the store and there was a short shelf of books on pets and pet care. She reached onto the shelf and pulled out a book on dogs.

'Joey, if you do really well in special ed,' she said, 'you can get a dog.'

And I was beaming inside. I had always wanted a dog. A little dog that looked just like me. A Joey dog. A nice, springy dog. A good dog. I had told Grandma I wanted one but she said having a dog in the house would be just like having two of me. But now I flipped through the book with a huge smile on my face. There were about a million dogs to chose from, but I knew which one was for me. A Chihuahua.

'Thanks,' I said. 'I'm not thinking bad thoughts.'

She knelt down and kissed me on the forehead. 'You better not be,' she replied. 'Your luck is changing. From now on you will be known as Joey Pigza, the lucky boy with his own dog.'

# 10.

# The Crossing

The next morning I was waiting on my front porch with my dog book when the blue-and-white handicapped bus for special ed pulled up. There was a loud hissing and suddenly the side door slapped open and a tiny platform lowered to the ground as the entire bus leaned to one side like an elephant kneeling down on one knee. I knew I was supposed to dash down the steps and hop on like a good boy, like Mom told me to do, but I just stood there and stared at it. There were small round mirrors on long steel poles stuck all over the corners of the bus. And from where I was standing, when I looked into the closest mirror, the whole world was stretched and curved so that I could see into the mirror on the back corner, and in that one I could see the other back mirror until I could see all the way around the bus and the front of the driver's face and the bald spot on the back of his head and actually see myself standing on my own porch with my backpack between my feet and my new short haircut Mom had given me after our walk. And as I looked at the little picture of myself in the mirror I wished I could see around the corner of this morning, into tomorrow and the next day, and find out in advance what was going to happen to me because even though I promised Mom I wouldn't think three bad thoughts in a row I felt I couldn't stop them if they showed up.

The driver flipped through some pages on a clipboard, then stood and opened the front door. 'Are you the new foster kid?' he called out, and it was a question that was very spooky to me, as if somehow going to special ed meant I was losing my mom too.

'I'm not a foster kid,' I said right back. 'I'm Joey Pigza. Who said I was a foster kid? I have a mom. She's just working. That doesn't mean I'm a foster kid.'

I could have kept on going because the more I talked the more upset I got. She was the only thing I had and it wasn't funny to have someone tease me that I was a foster kid. And while I was thinking about all this and standing as rigid as a locked door on the porch he looked down at the clipboard again and flipped over some more pages.

'Where's your mom?' he asked.

'I told you she's working,' I replied.

'Where?' he asked.

But I wouldn't tell him because I could hear the screeching sounds of his radio inside the cab and I thought if I told him he'd call someone and they'd take her away and it would be my fault that we didn't have each other any more because I cut off Maria's nose tip and people blamed her for not controlling me. Or maybe they already took her away and that's why I was being called a 'foster child'.

'Well, come on,' he said. 'We have a schedule to keep.'

I put my dog book in my backpack and walked down the steps. Not because I wanted to. I just didn't have a choice. There were only four other kids on the bus but I wished I had been picked up first so I could get used to them one at a time. Even though I had seen kids with some pretty awful problems in Mrs Howard's class, this was different. In Mrs Howard's class I always felt it was all of *them* and me, that I was special because I was better. But on the bus it was *us* and it made me think that I was special because I was as messed up as everyone else. First, there was a kid with no arms. Actually, he had arms but they were tiny and sticking straight out from his shoulders like fleshy pink brussels sprouts with twiggy little fingers stuck on the ends. The arms were so short he didn't even have elbows, and the sleeves of his T-shirt had been cut off so they wouldn't get covered up.

'Hi,' he said while his fingers scratched at the air like the legs on a turned-over crab. He gave me a head nod to sit next to him, so I did.

'Hi,' I said right back, and thought my medication might have been a dud because even though it was early in the morning when I was usually good I felt a surge of high-voltage willies flash through me. It was all I could do to sit down and squeeze my shoulders together toward the middle of my chest. I didn't want him to touch me. Still, when the bus lurched forward I fell against his hand and felt his tiny sharp fingernails scratching at my shirt.

'My name is Charlie,' he said, and I just looked at him from the neck up and it was OK.

'Joey,' I said in return. He leaned way forward as if he had dropped something on the floor and then his little hand touched my hand and I knew he wanted to shake because we had just met so I slipped my hand between his fingers and gave them a gentle tug.

'Nice to meet you,' he said when he sat up. 'What's your problem?'

'Nothing,' I said. 'Nothing at all except I think they're trying to take my mom away from me because he called me a foster kid.'

'They aren't going to take your mom away,' he said. 'I *begged* them to take mine and they wouldn't, so it's doubtful they'll take yours behind your back.'

I lost track of what he was saying because a kid was bumping his head against the back of my seat. I spun around to see what he was up to. He was banging it pretty hard so it was good that he was wearing a helmet. It wasn't a bicycle or football helmet, but more like one of those streamlined motorcycle helmets, and he kept rocking back and forth and lifting his feet off the floor and slamming into the metal rim of my seat back, and when I could get a glimpse of his eyes behind the clear visor it seemed to me that they were wincing in pain, as if a giant rock had flattened him and he was constantly trying to wiggle out from under it.

In front of me were two girls who seemed like any two girls, dressed nicely in clean clothes with shiny red backpacks on their laps. I touched my nose and smiled at them because girls reminded me of Maria, and they smiled back. 'What's wrong with them?' I whispered to Charlie.

'They're sisters. They get help once a week because they read and write everything backwards.' He turned to the girls. 'Show him what you can do.'

One girl held up her backpack. YAM was spelled across the top. I thought it was pretty bad that someone was named after a type of potato. The other backpack had ENUJ.

'Her name is *May*,' Charlie said. 'The other is *June*. Do you get it?'

I looked at May. She was grinning. 'My sister and I can write notes back and forth to each other in backwards writing and people can't understand it,' she said. 'Pretty cool.'

'Can you talk backwards?' I asked.

'I wish,' May said.

'Maybe they'll teach us at special ed,' said June, and giggled. 'That is, after we learn how to read *forwards* writing.'

We stopped at the railway tracks and the driver opened the door to listen for trains, but it was as if he had opened the door to tease me, as if he were singing, 'Come on, Joey foster kid. Bet you can't jump out the door and escape. Bet you don't have the guts.' And I was sweating and my feet were vibrating like rockets just before take-off. I could dive out the bus door and run away and bounce off the walls all the way to Pittsburgh like my dad, or I could pull myself together like my mom and go to special ed and get help. It was as if my life was trapped between two words: *run* or *stay*. And just as that kid behind me kept banging his head on the seat, I kept banging my head on those words: *run* or *stay*. And because I didn't know which to do I thought of my mom, who had already pulled herself together, and now it was my turn. Just then the door closed and we jerked forward over the bumpy tracks. I let out my old breath and took a fresh one.

Then I began to get nervous all over again about my mom being taken away because thinking of her and how she would behave had just saved me from doing something stupid like jumping out a bus door and running away, so now I was even more afraid they were taking her.

We pulled up at a big old brick house and a kid was standing on the sidewalk.

'Are you the foster kid?' the bus driver asked.

'Yeah,' he said, in a real bad mood. 'So what?'

When he stomped onto the bus I looked at him and he didn't look much different than me, so I closed my eyes because it was too sad.

When the bus stopped I opened my eyes. We were in front of a new white building with dark tinted windows that looked like a bank or a fancy office. Shiny steel letters on the wall spelled out LANCASTER COUNTY SPECIAL EDUCATION CENTRE. We must have arrived late because there were only a few people waiting for us on the sidewalk.

'See you later,' Charlie said, and used his foot to lift up his book bag so he could reach it with his miniature hand. He ran off towards a set of wide doors that opened automatically to let him in. The girls ran right behind him. I got off and a big man came up to me.

'Are you Joey Pigza?' he asked. He was wearing khaki trousers, a white shirt, and a striped tie.

'Yeah,' I said.

'I'm Mr Ed Vanness,' he said. 'I'm your case-worker and you can call me Special Ed. Almost everyone does.'

'There's something I have to tell you,' I replied.

'First, let me tell you about the school,' Special Ed said, as the front doors parted to let us in. 'It is not a school as you know it, and definitely *not* a place where you go because no-one wants you or likes you any more. It is not a place for punishment.'

'That's because everyone here has already been punished,' I said, and pointed to a kid in metal braces struggling to get up a ramp. His arms and legs looked like he was made out of twisted-up pipe cleaners.

Special Ed waved to him. 'Hey, Jason!' he

hollered. 'Looking good, buddy!'

Jason grinned as he jerked his head over to one side and said something that sounded like a smudged-up word.

'*He* is a great kid,' Special Ed said to me. 'For him to climb that ramp is like you and me climbing Mount Everest.'

'Can I tell you something?' I asked.

'One minute,' he said, and guided me toward an open elevator door. 'I want to show you round so you can see that this is a place you come to when you need extra help to get back on track. *I* can give you the help you need, and when you do, you can leave. In your case you have to be here at least six weeks because you hurt someone.'

'It was an *accident*!' I said.

'Yes, it was,' he agreed. 'But we don't want to repeat it. We want you to learn to make better choices and go back to school. If you become a regular here it just means we didn't do our job. Quite frankly, we like the kids who *don't* want to be here.'

I didn't hear much of what he was saying because I still had to tell him something. 'The bus driver thought I was a foster kid,' I blurted out.

'That was a mistake,' replied Special Ed.

'I want to see my mom,' I said.

'We can't do that right now,' he replied. 'We have other things to do. I have to introduce you to some of the people who will be helping you.'

'Then can we see my mom?' I asked.

'We'll call her on the phone,' Special Ed said. 'I promise.'

The elevator made a loud buzzing sound and the door opened. We walked down a wide, bright hall with classrooms on either side. Still, it seemed more like a hospital than a school because it smelled more of medicine than food. A line of blind kids holding on to a rope with one hand and white canes with the other tapped their way down the opposite wall. There were kids in wheelchairs and ordinary-looking kids carrying books. Then there were kids who were not going to make it back to regular school. They were busted up, or deformed and strapped onto wooden boards, or just mentally not all there.

I must have been staring at them because Special Ed asked me what I imagined other kids thought of me. 'They don't know what to think,' I said. 'I look fine.'

'So they are guessing at what is wrong with you.'

'Yeah,' I said. 'But they don't know.'

'Why?' he asked.

'Can I call my mom now?' I asked.

'Did you take your meds this morning?' he asked instead of answering.

'Yes,' I said.

'Did you eat breakfast?'

'No. I'm never hungry until I'm real hungry and then I could eat a cow.'

'Well, for starters,' Special Ed said, 'you are going to have to learn to eat even when you aren't hungry. Think of it this way – you have to take a bath every day whether you need it or not.'

'I didn't take a bath today,' I said. 'Am I in trouble?'

'No, you are not in trouble. This is not about you being in trouble. *This*,' he said, waving his hands around to mean the entire building and people in it, 'this is about getting you better.'

'It was trouble that got me sent here,' I said.

'And staying out of trouble will get you out,' he shot back as if he had all the answers memorized.

He unlocked a door and we walked into his office.

'Before I sit down can I go to the toilet?' I asked.

'Sure,' he said, and pointed to a door on the other side of the room.

I didn't really have to go. I just wanted to be alone for a minute so I stood there and flushed the toilet. I had thought the special-ed school was going to be like a prison for bad kids. That had always worried me. But it didn't seem to be mean. I didn't feel like someone would beat me up. And Special Ed wasn't as scary as I thought the teachers would be. In fact nothing was scarier than me knowing something was wrong inside me, something I couldn't see silently eating away at me like termites, and it was going to ruin me even when I was being good. I was scary to myself.

I flushed the toilet again and opened the door. 'My grandmother said there is nothing that can make me better,' I said. 'She said our whole family is sick and nothing will help.'

'I'm sure your grandmother is a nice person,' he said.

'She tried to put me in the refrigerator,' I blurted out.

'Sometimes nice people make bad decisions, Joey,' he said. 'I'm telling you, you will be fine. We're going to give you tests. We will determine if the meds you are taking are right for you. We'll make sure you are getting the right amount. We will help you feel better about yourself. We will help you get caught up on your homework. And we will both see that Joey Pigza is OK. And when you are, back to ordinary school you go.'

'Can I have a dog?' I asked.

He smiled. 'I think a dog is a very good idea,' he said. 'Do you know how to take care of one?'

'Not yet,' I said.

'Well, when you learn how to take care of a dog, you will have learned how to take care of yourself.'

'My grandma said I was part dog,' I said.

'I'd like to meet her,' Special Ed said. 'Really.'

'Well you can't,' I replied. 'She fell down into the sewers and was washed away.'

'Is that true?' he asked, and smiled real hard at me.

'She's in Pittsburgh with my dad. Can I call my mom now?' I asked.

He turned his phone round and pushed it towards me. I dialed the number. 'Beauty and the Beast hair salon,' answered Tiffany, the receptionist.

'This is Joey,' I said. 'Can I speak with my mom?'

'She's busy with a customer,' she said. 'Can I leave a message?'

'I'll call back,' I said, and hung up. Then I instantly called again, because sometimes that's what I do until Tiffany gets Mom.

'She's still not available,' Tiffany said. 'We've talked about this calling binge, Joey. Now give it a rest before you call again.'

I hung up and began to dial again but Special Ed pushed the dial-tone button and cut me off. 'Joey,' he said, 'it's time we had a very serious talk.'

'Can I get back to you on that?' I replied, and began to feel itchy in my seat.

'There is a serious reason why you are here,' he said. 'Simply put, you hurt another student and until we are certain you won't hurt someone else then you can't go back. That's the bottom line, Joey. Do you see what I mean?'

'If Mrs Howard hadn't made me wear the

rabbit slippers,' I answered, 'I wouldn't have tripped and cut Maria's nose off.'

'It's not the slippers, Joey,' he said.

'Then what?' I asked. 'What?'

'It's how you make decisions.'

'Like what?'

'You stuck your finger in a pencil sharpener. You swallowed a key. You lost it at the field trip, Joey, you make very bad decisions for yourself.'

'I got dud meds,' I said. 'They work in the morning and don't after lunch.'

'We can help with the meds,' Special Ed said. 'But that is the easiest part. You still have to learn how to make good decisions.'

I picked up the phone and started to dial. 'I want my mom,' I said.

He pressed the dial-tone button. 'What if I told you your home life is part of the problem? We have to get serious now, Joey. It's time to look at the big picture.'

## 11.

# Shifting Gears

I was bouncing an orange tennis ball against the front door as I sat on the porch. I did it over and over for about an hour. I wasn't locked out. I was just waiting for Mom. When I saw her turn the corner on Queen Street about five houses down I just kept throwing the ball harder and harder until she started up the sidewalk. Then I turned and let it all out.

'He said you were part of the big picture problem,' I shouted. 'I said *I* cut Maria's nose off, not you. And he said this was not all about Maria's nose. This was about how I make decisions. I told him I had dud meds and he wanted to know what doctors you had taken me to. I told him I didn't know and that you rescued me from Grandma and he said special ed was going to help me get better. What does that mean?'

'Calm down. You don't have to shout, and stop picking at your head,' she said, and glanced over her shoulder to see if the neighbours were listening. 'Let's go inside and take some medicine and talk about it. And who is *he* anyway?'

'Special Ed,' I replied.

'Oh, yeah. The guy with the two names,' she muttered.

We went into the house and I kept talking but Mom didn't listen. 'This place is a mess,' she said, and shook her head. 'What have you been doing?'

'I was flippin' out,' I said. 'The bus driver called me a foster child and I thought they had taken you away because of what I had done to Maria. I called you at work but you wouldn't come to the phone. So I kept calling but Tiffany said you were unavailable and I thought they'd arrested you instead of me. Then later, I thought you got sick of me and ran off again. And I told that to Special Ed and he said that my home life was a big part of my problem.'

'You told me you were not going to tear the house apart looking for your meds,' she said.

'I had a bad day,' I said.

'We *all* have bad days,' she replied. 'You just have to deal with them.'

Mom reached into her purse and took out the plastic vial of medicine for me. She shook one pill into her hand. 'You didn't leave a number where you could be reached. Otherwise I would have called you back.' She slipped half a pill between my lips.

After I swallowed I went to the refrigerator to get her the Mountain Dew as she pulled the Amaretto out from under the sink. She mixed herself a drink and I dropped a red cherry into it.

'So he said I'm to blame?' she asked after a minute.

'He wanted to know how I felt after you abandoned me.'

'I left you with your grandmother.'

'She was mean,' I said. 'And I told that to Special Ed too.'

'What else did you tell him?'

'About Dad.'

'And?'

'About our days. From when I wake up to when I go to bed. Everything.'

'Did you tell them I love you and I go to work every day at the beauty parlour and listen to everyone talk about their perfect kids and how sick that makes me because for one, I don't believe their kids are perfect because no-one is, and two, they pretend their kids are perfect so they can look down at kids like you and parents like me.'

She stood up and made another Amaretto sour.

'If you have two drinks does that mean I can have two meds?'

'No. It does not. And I wish you wouldn't go round telling strangers what we do at home.'

'Special Ed said he's here to help me and that things would get worse before they'd get better.'

'He's right on that score,' she said. 'Damn right. You can tell him things might get worse for him too.' And she drank that drink down like it was water and mixed another while I just stared at her.

'No. Don't tell him that,' she said, calming down. 'It was a bad day for me too. I thought about you at work all day and I worried about you and the more I thought about what you would tell them about us the more embarrassed I was. I came back for you, but just coming back isn't good enough. It's not just about having a roof over our heads, it's about what is in our heads. Do you get what I'm saying?'

'Yeah,' I said. 'I spoke with a diet lady today and she said I don't eat right for my body too.'

'Now, what did you tell *her*?' Mom asked, and she lost her cool again.

'That I like chocolate doughnut holes and French fries and nachos and that you never make me eat what I don't like.'

'And what is wrong with that?'

'She said I need vegetables and salads and grains and asked if I take vitamins. I told her I eat a Reese's peanut-butter cup every morning because you said peanut butter was good for me.'

'I need another drink,' she said.

'Special Ed asked me if you drink,' I said.

She whipped around with the Amaretto bottle in her hand. 'And what did you tell him?'

'That you drink,' I said. 'You do.' I pointed

at the bottle in her hand. 'See? And Special Ed said that if I didn't tell the truth I wouldn't get better.'

'Well, I spoke with Mr Vanness today,' she said, and mixed the drink.

'It's the same guy,' I said. 'He's Special Ed.'

'I know,' she said. 'He called me after you left his office.'

'What did he say?'

'I'm not telling,' she said. 'That's one of the differences between you and me. I know how to keep my mouth shut.'

'I can't help it that I talk too much,' I said.

'Try,' she said.

'Try not drinking,' I said.

'Why is it that one of us has to be right and one of us has to be wrong?' she asked. '*Why* does it always come down to that?'

'Don't ask me *why*,' I said, and pushed my fingers in my ears not to hear the word.

She pulled my hands away. 'Sometimes you really get under my skin,' she said. 'Sometimes I think it was easier chasing after your dad than it is chasing after you.'

'But you love me more,' I said. 'You said so yourself.'

'You are such an imp,' she growled.

I just smiled my big smile, the one where my eyes close up and I can't see anything but the inside of my face, which is like wearing a great big Halloween yellow smiley face mask.

'Come on,' she said. 'Let's be bad for another day and order a pizza.'

'Can we get vegetables on it?' I asked. 'I promised I'd eat more.'

'Yeah. Like what? Mushrooms, green peppers, onions?'

'Don't forget the salad.'

'Get real,' she said. 'They don't make salad pizza. Salad is the opposite of pizza. Salad is for rabbits and pizza is for people who *love* cheese and sausage and pepperoni. And that happens to be us.'

In the morning I was sitting in the porch eating a slice of leftover extra-cheese-and-vegetable pizza and waiting for the bus when Mrs Maxy pulled up in her car and waved to me. And she was smiling, too, which was a good thing or I would have turned right around and dashed into the house and locked the door. When she got out of her car she was carrying a brown paper bag and her handbag.

'How is it going?' she asked as she climbed the steps.

'Pretty good,' I said. 'Now that I'm eating more vegetables. Wanna bite?'

'No, thanks,' she replied, and shook her head at me just like my mom does. 'We've all been thinking of you.'

That made me feel a lot better than pizza. 'I think of you too,' I replied. 'And I'll be back. I told you I would.'

'Well, keep making progress and I'm sure you will.'

I got my courage up to ask the next question. 'How's Maria?' I asked. 'I went to her house to say I was sorry and her dad chased me away.'

'Maria is no longer at our school,' Mrs Maxy said. 'Her family sent her to the Catholic school.'

'We have kids from the Catholic school in special ed,' I said. 'They still wear their uniforms.'

'I know,' said Mrs Maxy. 'We told her parents that the accident could have happened anywhere but they were very concerned for Maria.'

'I still feel real bad about what happened,' I said.

'We all do, Joey,' Mrs Maxy said. 'But we have to get over it and move on. Now, let me show you what I've brought.' She removed a folder from the bag and showed me my math, English, geography, history, and science lessons. 'Do these here with your mom and you can keep up with the class for the next few weeks. I'll keep bringing your homework so when they send you back you won't be too far behind. OK?'

'Does this mean they are sending me back in six weeks?' I asked.

'That is up to someone else,' she said. 'But Mr Vanness called and asked me to keep up with your assignments so if and when you do come back you can jump right in.'

Then before she left I said, 'I'm sorry.'

'I know you are, Joey. We all are. But we can stop being sorry now. It's time to shift gears and make sure it doesn't happen again. OK?'

'I'm sorry,' I said again. I held my arms out for a hug and she gave me one and it was really good and when I let go of her I said, 'I'm shifting gears and making certain it won't happen again.'

'Good,' she said. 'Very good.' And she

reached into her teacher bag and pulled out a strip of sticky gold stars. She peeled one off and pressed it onto my forehead. 'This,' she said, 'is for shifting gears.'

I carefully touched the star and felt the five gold points. One for each subject. 'My mom said when I'm better she'll get me a dog.'

'That would be very nice,' she said. 'I have to run. You know how the class can get when I'm not there on time.'

I remembered.

She turned and walked down the steps and I could see pizza sauce on the back of her dress where I had put my hands during our hug.

'Mrs Maxy!' I hollered and waved the pizza in the air.

'I already packed a lunch,' she called back, before I could tell her about the hand prints. 'Thanks.'

As soon as she left I wiped my hands on my trousers and dumped all the stuff she brought me inside the house. In a few minutes the special-ed bus pulled up. I got on and Charlie was waiting for me.

'Sit here,' he said, and gave me a head nod just like yesterday.

'Want some pizza?' I asked.

'Sure,' he said, and I held it up to his mouth and he took a bite.

'Be careful,' I said. 'It's a little messy.'

It was a big day and it wasn't going well. It was my turn to see the doctor and I think that had me all over-excited. I had taken my meds in the morning but I still couldn't keep my mind on my work. I had a reading teacher who made me read picture books instead of chapter books because she said the pictures would help me understand the words that were beyond my reading level. But I just wasn't paying attention. Then in math I couldn't do my drills because inside my head were loud scary doctor thoughts and I couldn't seem to hear the teacher. Break time was about the best thing to do because I could just run around the swing set while dodging between the kids who swung back and forth like wrecking balls trying to knock my block off.

Finally, at the end of the day, I was sitting in a small examination room with Special Ed and he was looking at his watch. There was a cabinet next to me with a lot of neat stuff inside. I opened it and took out the Band-Aids.

'Joey,' Special Ed said, 'put those back.'

'I was just looking at them. There's no harm in that.'

'While we are waiting,' he said in his fake doctor voice, 'I think we should talk about something important.'

'Yeah,' I said. 'Grandma always said not to waste time with the little stuff.'

'The doctor is going to be concerned with your physical condition and your medication,' he said. 'That is his job. My job is to be concerned about your behaviour, which is why we have to be a team. Long after the doctor gets your medication regulated, you and I will be working together.'

'I think I've had very good behaviour,' I said. 'I haven't been in trouble for days.'

'That is good,' he said. 'But we need to do more than just *avoid* getting into trouble. We need to focus on *how* to make the right decisions so you aren't in trouble in the first place.'

'What does that mean?'

'The Band-Aids, Joey,' he said, pointing to the cabinet. 'If I left you here alone for a few minutes what would you do with them?'

'Nothing.'

'Nothing?' he said, doubting me.

'Nothing,' I said again.

'Then let's test that out,' he said, and stood up. 'I'll be out in the hall.'

As soon as the door closed I began to rip open the Band-Aids right away. I pulled up my T-shirt and started sticking them all over my chest and belly. I must have got about twenty of them on when I heard Special Ed say, 'Good morning, doctor.' I quickly hid the wrappers on the windowsill behind the curtain, pulled my shirt down over my belly, and took my seat.

The door opened and the doctor rushed in.

'I'm Dr Preston,' he said. 'Sorry I'm late. My fault.'

I liked him right away because, for once, what went wrong wasn't *my* fault.

He set his briefcase on the table and removed his jacket. 'Is Mrs Pigza joining us?' he asked, first looking at me, then at Special Ed, who had taken his seat.

'She couldn't make it at this time,' Special Ed replied. 'But we've spoken and I'll keep her informed.'

The doctor pursed his lips. 'Right,' he said dryly. As if he were thinking, 'Wrong.' As if he were thinking my whole life was wrong and it started with my mom because she didn't care enough about me to make it here.

'Well,' he said, smiling again. 'Here's what we are going to do.' He snapped open his brief-case and removed my file. 'First, I'm going to give you a quick check-up. Then we're going to run some tests. Not awful tests, but we have to draw blood and you have to pee in a cup.'

It didn't sound too bad. 'I've had to do worse things,' I said. 'One time I was with Grandma on a bus and she made me pee in a Coke bottle.'

'I get the picture,' Dr Preston said as he opened my file and looked at what was written as intensely as if he had just cut open my chest and was watching all my organs work.

When he looked up he took a deep breath, then started talking. 'You seem like a nice, smart kid so I'm going to be honest and give you both the easy news and the hard news, Joey. We all feel that the meds you're taking now aren't doing the job and with better medication your attention disorder can be controlled. That part we can manage. But the hard part for us is determining just the right medication. The written tests and the question-and-answer tests help us chart your behaviour. You know, can't sit still, have trouble concentrating, stray from your tasks and all. I wouldn't tell you this so bluntly unless you didn't know it already. And I know you and Mr Vanness have talked about this.'

I wanted to tell him that I had talked with every teacher I had ever known about just this same stuff. But Special Ed had told me earlier to let the doctor talk and my job was to listen, so I chewed on the inside of my left cheek because I had chewed up the inside of my right one the day before and it still hurt.

'What I'm getting at is this. What we don't know is what, medically speaking, is going on inside of you. And that we need to know before we can get you the proper medication. So here is what we are going to do. I want you to go to the Children's Hospital in Pittsburgh and get a test. It sounds scarier than it is. It's called a brain SPECT test. They take pictures of your brain, kind of like X-rays only a lot more detailed and in colour. The test does not hurt one bit.'

'Is there something wrong with my brain?' I asked. 'Because I've seen a lot of people around here with sick brains and they don't look right or act right.'

Special Ed jumped in. 'The doctor is saying he just wants to get the test so he can make sure nothing else is wrong before he gives you the *right* kind of medicine and the right amount.'

'Exactly,' said Dr Preston.

'Can my mom come?'

'Absolutely,' the doctor said. 'In fact, she has to.'

'I don't think she can get off work,' I said, and looked at Special Ed. 'She works a lot.'

'We'll see to it,' Special Ed said. 'Don't worry.'

'Joey,' the doctor said as he pulled a stethoscope out of his pocket. 'I want to listen to your heart. Sit up here,' and he patted the edge of the examination table that was covered with a sheet of paper.

I glanced over at Special Ed and was going to tell him about the Band-Aids but he just looked at me as if he was so proud of me. Like he was a really good dad, so I hopped up on the table and took a seat.

When Dr Preston lifted my shirt his face got really worried and he lowered my shirt again.

'Mr Vanness,' he said seriously, 'may I speak with you out in the hall?'

As soon as they were gone I began to peel off the Band-Aids but I only had a few off before Special Ed shot back into the room. 'Joey,' he said in a very strict voice. The doctor was right behind him. 'Explain to the doctor what you did.'

I looked at him. 'I decorated my belly with Band-Aids,' I said. 'What's the big deal?'

'The doctor thought you had been abused,' Special Ed said in the same tight voice. 'That's the big deal.'

'No way,' I said. 'Nobody has beat me up since Grandma did it with a fly-swatter.'

The doctor continued his examination, then turned to Special Ed. 'I'm finished for now. Have the nurse fill in his chart,' he said, 'and run the blood and urine tests.' Then he stepped over to the desk and closed his brief-case. 'I'm sorry to be in such a hurry, Joey. But until I get all those test results I can't make a decision as regards medication, and there are a lot of ways to go.' I stood up and he shook my hand and I looked right into his eyes because Mom told me that if you look into a person's eyes you can tell if they are lying or not.

'Am I OK?' I said. His eyes stayed right on mine. They didn't slide left or right or blink and roll back or do something else like look at the door or his watch.

'My feeling is that you will be OK. You do have a medical problem. You also have some behaviour problems. I think both of those problems can be managed. I think your brain is fine. You have slugged it out for a long while and now you've hit the wall. You couldn't have done that if something was seriously wrong. We're doing the test just to be on the safe side.'

'I'm only asking because it's my brain and I need to know and I'll see my mom and she'll want to know too.'

Special Ed stood up and nodded to the doctor. 'I'll take care of this end of things,' he said. 'And keep you posted.'

'Bye, Joey,' the doctor said. 'I'll see you as soon as we get the results from the tests.' Then he opened the door and I could hear him marching down the hallway.

I just waved at where he had been as if suddenly I was only two years old and didn't know 'hello' and 'goodbye' and would wave no matter if I was coming or going. And I wanted to keep looking at the door because I figured as soon as I turned round, Special Ed was going to get on me about the Band-Aids. But he didn't even ask about them. Instead he put his hand on my shoulder.

'How are you holding up?' he said.

I was trying to be hopeful. To look on the bright side as Mom said. But thinking that there was something wrong with my brain was scaring me. I had already seen so many kids with bad brains and the worst part is that some of them looked just like me. Looked normal. But like me, there was something wrong inside.

'I'm not doing so good,' I said. I was going to say that I was scared, but I had said that so many times already that I thought it was dumb to keep saying the same thing over and over as if my brain wasn't working right.

'Do you want to call your mom?' he asked, and picked up the phone. He had already dialled the number by the time I said yes.

## 12.

# Pittsburgh

After I had talked to Mom, Special Ed spoke with her about going the next day to the hospital in Pittsburgh. When she came home from work that night she had a new slacks-and-shirt outfit for me, but it was for the hospital visit. 'I want you to look good,' she said, and examined my head. 'I always feel my best when I look good.'

Early the next morning when it was still dark we got all cleaned up and I dressed in my old jeans and a Penn State T-shirt for the bus ride. I took my meds and Mom drank coffee while she made sandwiches and packed them in our travel bags. By then the taxi was blowing its horn and once we got in it took us to the bus station. We were the first in line. After the driver opened the passenger door, we went up the steps. I had been on school buses and city buses, and of course the special-ed bus, but I had never been on a big Greyhound bus before and I was very excited not just because it was a bus but because it was named after a dog.

We had our choice of where to sit. I wanted to sit all the way at the back and have the whole long seat.

'No,' Mom said. 'The toilet is back there.' She pointed at the tiny silver room. 'And they smell funny. Get a spot in the middle for the best ride.'

'How do you know?'

'Your dad and I took a lot of buses,' she said. 'We went to Harrisburg, Pittsburgh, Philadelphia, Baltimore, all over. He was always on the move.'

'Do you think he's in Pittsburgh?' I asked.

'Honey, he could be on the moon. I just don't know,' she said in a voice that didn't want to talk about it.

'But if he is . . .'

'Don't get your hopes up about bumping into your father, Joey,' she said. 'He wouldn't know you if he saw you.'

It hurt to think he wouldn't know me from any other kid so I tried not to think about him or even Grandma. Already I had enough scary thoughts to worry me about my brain being messed up so I tried to think of something good like Mom told me to do. Just one good thing. I leaned my head against the glass and fell asleep. That was the best I could do.

When I woke up, Mom wanted to know if I was hungry. I was, so she got the food and I opened the dog book which I had brought with me.

'Don't you think you should do your homework first?' she asked, but it was more of an order.

'After we eat,' I begged. 'Then you can help me.'

'OK,' she said, and spread out the paper towels and sandwich on her lap. 'But no tricks. You have to keep up like Mrs Maxy said.'

I flipped through the pages of dogs. 'I like this one,' I said, pointing at a Chinese crested.

'It only has fur on the tip-top of its head,' she said. 'Like a troll doll.'

I didn't care about that. 'This is the puppy I really want,' I said, and pointed at a brown Chihuahua.

'Is there a Joey puppy in there?' she asked, then leaned over to kiss me and tried to be sneaky and check my bald spot again.

'I know how to be your puppy,' I said, and jerked my head away. 'After you were gone I started asking Grandma when you were coming back and she said, "Any day now, I suspect." And she put a chair in the front-room window and every evening I would sit there with my toys and stuffed animals and books and I'd wait. Grandma wouldn't let me out of my chair so I stood on it, kneeled on the seat, scraped it around backward, and rode it like a horse, and all the time I kept my eye on the sidewalk looking for you and every now and again a woman selling cookies or magazines or church raffle tickets would come up the sidewalk and I'd spring forward and flatten my face against the glass window, but I didn't know what to look for 'cause I didn't remember what you looked like, remember? So I yelled out to Grandma, "Is that my mom?"'

'Joey,' Mom said, 'is this going to be about Grandma treating you badly?'

'Yes,' I said.

'You've told me this before and it hurts me to hear it over and over,' she said.

So I shut up. But it was the kind of story that doesn't go away after the first time you tell it so you have to tell it over and over until it goes away for good. If it ever can. I looked out of the window and thought of Special Ed and acted in my mind like I was speaking to him because I hadn't told him yet but planned to.

Grandma would tease me all the time while I waited at the window for Mom. 'Look at you,' she'd say. 'You're like a little puppy.' And she made me do puppy tricks.

'Roll over,' she'd command, and I'd get on the floor and roll over and over until I bumped into the wall. 'Sit up!' she'd shout, and clap her hands, and I would, with my little arms up in front of my face and my wrists curled down like paws. 'Bark,' she'd say, and if I didn't she'd get the fly-swatter and swat me across the bottom until I sounded like a pet store full of dogs. There was one command I did like. 'Beg!' she'd snap, and I'd begin to whine like a dog going, 'Pleeeease, pleeeease,

'pleeeease,' until she'd give me a hard candy that she'd swiped by the handful from the fish-bowl of free candy at the bank where she cashed her Social Security cheque. I loved that candy and I'd beg and beg until I got it all.

Sometimes she'd get so mad at me for not being good she'd pretend that the phone rang and she'd hold it to her ear and say, 'Yes. Why yes. Oh, that is so wonderful that you are coming home. When? Tonight? Oh, Joey will be so excited. So excited.'

And I was. I'd be pulling on the phone cord trying to get the receiver so I could yell 'hurry up' into it, but Grandma would hold it tight and stiff-arm me with her other hand and then she'd say, 'What? You want him to take a bath then sit nice and still and not fidget in his seat? OK. We'll try.' Then she'd set the receiver down and I'd pick it up and yell, 'Mom!' into it but she had already hung up. 'Now don't let your mom down,' Grandma would say, and I'd run to the bathroom and scrub myself red and when I was perfectly clean I'd put on my pyjamas and sit in the window chair and if I'd wiggle just a little tiny bit Grandma would say from across the room where she was doing crossword puzzles, 'See, I just saw her walk by and she saw that you were not sitting still and she just kept on walking 'cause your mom does not want to come home to a bad boy.'

'That's not true!' I'd scream. And I'd get so nervous I'd pull my hair out. Not fistfuls, but one little hair at a time until I had round bald patches on my head. I knew it was bad, but I couldn't help it, and then Grandma would pick up the phone again and say, 'What? You aren't coming back until he learns not to pull his hair out like an idiot? OK, I'll tell him.' Then she'd hang up and say to me, 'Did you hear that, Joey?' And by then I'd be crying and crying because I hated myself so much for not being able to sit still and keep my hands in my lap, and then Grandma would say into the phone again, 'But you are willing to try again tomorrow night. Oh, that is so nice of you, dear. You are a saint to love this boy the way you do. I'll see to it that he is in the chair by the window. Yes, I'll tell him that you'll be passing by to check on him and if he is sitting still you will come knock on the door.'

So the next night I'd start off sitting in the chair twiddling my thumbs and when any woman walked down the sidewalk I'd straighten up and sit real still but when the woman passed by I'd slump back because there I was being good, but for the wrong woman. And I waved and smiled so much at strange women that once I was playing on the front porch and a woman passed by and pointed at me and said to her kid, 'Look there is that nice boy who sits in the window and waves to everyone.' So I waved back and her daughter said, 'What's wrong with his head?' Because I had those little shiny spots that looked like holes.

I turned away from staring out the bus window and from thinking about Grandma and the past and looked at Mom, who was filing her nails. 'Can I talk to you again?' I asked.

'Only if you tell me something new,' she said.

'OK. One of the reasons I want a puppy is because it will wait in the window for me every day and every day I will come home to it. You didn't come home to me but I promise I'll come home to it. I'll take care of it because I don't want it to feel like I did. So if the test on my brain is good then I should get a puppy because of a celebration, and if the test is bad I should get one because you have to be really nice to me because then it'll be proven that I'm messed up in the head and nobody can fix it. Either way, I should get a dog.'

When I finished talking her head was tilted forward against the back of the next seat, because everything I said was all in her brain like a heavy weight and she had to rest it for a minute. But I didn't care. Special Ed said that I might get mad at her some day and he was right.

'So *why*, after all I put you through, do you still love me?' she finally said, and slipped the nail file into her purse. '*Why?*'

'I don't know *why*,' I said. 'I just do. You're my mom and I do. Anyway, you love me and I'm messed up in the head for life.'

'Don't think that,' she said, and kissed me on the side of the face, then began to straighten my shirt and push back my hair as if looking better would mean I was better.

'And the puppy?' I asked.

'I think you know that once we get back home we can get one.'

'Yes!' I said, and pumped my fist. 'Yes! 'Cause Maria has one and I don't want to have to wait until someone cuts off my nose to get one.'

'I'm sure Maria is a very nice girl,' Mom said. 'So no more silly talk about her. OK?'

'OK,' I said, and began to flip through the dog book again.

'We'll find a cure for you, Joey,' Mom said.

'No you won't,' I replied. 'There is no cure.'

'Well, you're not doomed,' she said sarcastically.

'I know,' I said. 'But there is no cure. The doctor and Special Ed said so.'

'I don't mean *cure* like you take a pill and it all goes away,' she said.

'Then say what you mean,' I said, and I could feel myself slipping away because suddenly I didn't want to sit in my seat and everything outside the window became really blurry and I could feel my brain getting stuck on one thought. 'You know what I mean? Say what you mean. You know what I mean?' I said again as if repeating that thought would give me a running head start into getting the next thought going. But I was stuck in a rut. 'You know what I mean?' I repeated, a little louder and a little meaner. 'You know what I *mean*!'

'Come on,' Mom whispered, and grabbed my hand. 'Let's go to the toilet for just a minute.'

She pulled me out of the seat and tightened her grip on my hand as she dragged me down the aisle, and I kept bouncing from side and side and touching some people.

'Sorry,' Mom kept saying to them. 'Sorry.'

And for a second I thought, She is sorry. She is always sorry.

When we got to the toilet it was so small. Mom opened the door and sat down on the toilet lid and I leaned in over her. She pulled the door closed against my butt and latched it, then unzipped her bag. She took out my medicine and I opened my mouth.

'Be my good little baby bird,' she said quietly, and slipped the pill onto my tongue.

We stayed that way and as the bus rumbled down the road it felt like the whole planet was loose and was bouncing down a long flight of steps.

'I have a confession to make,' Mom finally said.

'What?'

'There was a time when I wanted to be with you but I wasn't in shape to return. I was drinking with your father and wasn't taking good care of myself. So when I decided to return I would walk by the house and try to see you because it would give me extra strength to pull myself together. But I swear, I never saw you sitting in the window and I never knew what Grandma was making you do.'

I put my cheek down on the top of her head and smelled her hair. Because she had so many beauty supplies it always smelled sweet and creamy. We stayed that way until the bus stopped and the driver knocked on the door.

'Pittsburgh,' he said. 'Come on out.'

## 13.

# MOON MAN

My test was over within a few minutes after we arrived at the hospital. First, we got into an elevator and off at Radiology. Mom went up to the woman at the desk and was given some papers to fill out while a nurse came for me. 'When you finish up the paperwork,' she said to Mom, 'we'll be in room number three.'

As soon as we walked into the examination room I spotted the glass jar of Band-Aids. 'Can I have one?' I asked.

'Sure,' she said, and opened the jar herself, then slipped just one into my top pocket. Before I could ask for another she put the jar up on the top shelf. 'Now undress and put this on,' she instructed, and gave me a thin white robe.

'But my outfit's new,' I said. 'I just put it on after the bus ride.'

She smiled. 'Don't worry. We'll keep an eye on it. And I want you to put this rubber mouthpiece between your teeth and bite down really hard. We'll need you to keep your jaw and teeth clenched so we can keep your head real still while we take the pictures.'

'But I got my new outfit for the picture,' I said.

'It's not that kind of picture,' she said.

'OK,' I answered, because this time I didn't want to do anything wrong.

'I'll get everything ready,' she said, and half stepped out the door. 'Just remember, this won't hurt and it won't take long. Lots of kids have done it. It's a breeze. The most important thing is to lie still.'

As soon as she was gone I pushed a chair over to the stack of shelves, hopped up, and opened the jar. I grabbed a handful of Band-Aids and stuffed them into my pocket. Then I hopped down, put the chair away, and changed into the robe.

After that everything happened so quickly I didn't have time to make mistakes. The nurse took me into a bright room and helped lift me onto a table. She made me lie on my back and all the time she kept squeezing my arms and legs and shoulders into place as if I were made out of Silly Putty until I was just the right shape.

'Now hold still and play like an Egyptian mummy,' she said. 'Don't even wiggle your eyes.'

I closed them, and could hear her quickly walking away. A door closed on the other side of the room and soon the machine that takes the pictures began to buzz, then slowly it passed over me. And when it did my brain tingled as if it were a honeycomb full of bees. I always liked bees and honey and it made me feel better to think of bees than being some old dead mummy with a dried-up walnut brain. Suddenly the buzzing stopped, and it was finished.

A door opened and I heard footsteps coming my way. 'You can open your eyes now,' the nurse said. 'And wiggle your eyeballs.' She reached into my mouth, pulled out the rubber mouthpiece, and put it in a small white bag.

'Hop up. You were great. No twitching, no coughing or sneezing. You're a real pro at being still.'

I grinned. 'I must be getting better already,' I said.

'Yep,' she replied. 'Now, come along.'

Mom was waiting for me in the examination room. 'How'd it go?' she asked, and kissed me on the head.

'I think my brain is filled with bees,' I replied.

She got a crooked smile on her face. 'Don't make fun of your brain,' she said. 'It scares me.'

Because she was scared, then I got scared and wanted to get going. I quickly pulled my clothes back on and we said thank you and goodbye to everyone. As we walked away the nurse said the test results would be sent directly to the doctor. We didn't stop to talk about it. We got into the elevator and when the doors closed I felt much better.

'I don't like hospitals,' I said to Mom.

'That's why they have gift shops,' she said, and put one arm around me while her other arm held her travel bag.

'What can I buy?' I asked. 'What?'

'There are rules,' she reminded me. 'Just keep in mind my wallet is pretty skinny.'

We went into the gift shop and I could feel my head buzzing again. They had the coolest stuff I had ever seen. It's like they saved the best toys in the world just for the sick kids. There was a whole zoo of kid-sized stuffed animals. I pointed at the giraffe.

'Don't even think about it,' Mom said.

'How about the big battery-powered car I can drive?'

'Nope.'

'The humungous can of peanut brittle?'

'Nope.'

'What then? What?'

'Be reasonable, Joey,' she said. 'Choose something that can fit in your pocket.'

'You're supposed to feel sorry for me,' I said.

'What I feel for you and what I can afford are two different things,' she said. 'Besides, you'll be fine.'

'Fine,' I repeated, only in a different way, and stomped over to the revolving postcard rack. 'I'll just get a card,' I said loudly, making a fuss, but I didn't care. I wanted something nice because there was still a chance my brain looked more like scrambled eggs than a honeycomb.

'A card is a very nice souvenir,' she said

just like a mom because the saleslady was watching us as if we were house burglars.

I grabbed the wire postcard rack with one hand and spun it around as fast as I could just as some old lady was about to pluck one out, and I almost chopped her finger off. She gave me a startled look like the hoot owl at the Amish farm, then backed off towards a shelf of Beanie Babies. I kept spinning the rack faster and faster until it was a postcard tornado and the cards were sailing out of their holders and skidding across the floor.

'Joey!' Mom snapped, scolding me. 'Joey. Stop it.'

I wouldn't, but she did. She grabbed my arm with one hand and the wire rack with the other and it nearly toppled over but didn't. It just wobbled around in a circle like a drunk person. 'Now help me pick these up,' she ordered, bending over.

I got down on my hands and knees like a dog and put them in my mouth.

'Stop that,' she said, getting mad and yanking them out of my mouth. 'Nobody wants Joey slobber on their card.'

'I know what I want that will fit in my pocket,' I said.

'What?'

'A Chihuahua.'

'Can I get back to you on that?' she snapped.

Then the saleslady stood over us. 'May I help you?' she asked as if she wanted to help us right out the door.

'Do you sell Chihuahuas?' Mom asked.

'I'm afraid not,' the lady replied with a really fake smile on her face and then she began to tidy up the postcard rack.

'Then we'll just have to take our business someplace else,' Mom said, sounding snotty. She grabbed my arm and marched me across the lobby and out the door and we kept marching until we weren't really sure where we were.

After a few minutes Mom set her bag down and looked over at the bank clock. 'We've got some extra time to kill. Let's do some sight-seeing.'

'Yeah,' I said. 'We could go to the Igloo and see the Penguins.'

'I don't think they let you see the ice-hockey rink when they're not playing a game,' she said. 'Besides, I was thinking more about going up to the Sky Deck of the PPG building and seeing the whole city from one spot.'

'Do they have telescopes?'

'I would think so,' she said. But she wasn't sure so I started hoping they did right away because there was something more inside my mind buzzing around besides bees. I had an idea about what I wanted to find in Pittsburgh.

When we arrived at the PPG building we took the elevator up about fifty floors and by then Mom looked pale.

'I think I'm going to be seasick,' she said as we stepped out and walked toward the line of telescopes by the big windows. She sat down and took a deep breath.

'I need a quarter,' I said. 'For the telescope.'

She reached into her bag and gave me one. I stood up on a little metal stool and slipped it into the slot and looked through the eyehole. I aimed the telescope way up into the air, about as far away from Pittsburgh as you could get.

'What are you looking for?' she asked.

'The moon,' I said. 'You said Dad might be living up there.'

'Is this why you wanted to come up here? To look for him?'

'Coming up here was your idea,' I said, and

166

aimed the telescope at her. 'Smile,' I said. But I couldn't tell if she was, because she was too close and everything was blurry.

I lowered the telescope down to the street and watched people walk up and down the streets. Any one of those guys could have been my dad. 'Can we call him on the phone?' I asked.

'Don't try and pull something over on me, Joey,' she said. 'We're not here to look for him.'

'I'm just asking,' I said. 'I'd like to meet him.'

'I don't think so,' she said. 'I don't think you'd like him.'

'Remember,' I said, 'before you returned, Grandma talked bad about you and said I wouldn't like you either. But then when you came back I began to like you. It could be the same with Dad. Maybe if I met him I'd like him too.'

'Take my word for it,' she said. 'You won't.'

'Maybe not,' I said. 'But I won't know for sure until I meet him.' I looked through the telescope again.

'You better look into the bars,' she said. 'If you see some nervous little guy with a drunk red piggy-Pigza face, that'll be him.'

'Do people call him names too?' I asked.

'Don't start feeling sorry for him,' she said. 'He just goes around asking for trouble.'

'Maybe he stopped drinking,' I said.

'Yeah. And birds stopped flying,' she replied sarcastically.

'There is nothing wrong with wanting to meet my own dad,' I said.

The meter on the telescope ran out and everything went black. When I looked at her she said, 'I don't have another quarter.'

I stepped off the stool and started walking across the room towards the phone book at the pay phone. 'I can look his name up,' I said as she hopped up and followed.

'I know you'd like to meet your father,' she said. 'I know it would be good for you to meet him. What troubles me is how *he'll* be. He could be drunk, he could be sober, he could be nice, or mean as a snake. If I knew he had settled down, then we'd think about getting together. But until I know that for sure I can't take a chance that he won't upset you more than love you. Do you understand that?'

I flipped through the phone book to the P section. Then I turned the pages and went up and down the list of names with my finger. There was no Carter Pigza, or Grandma Pigza.

'Well?' she asked. 'Are you satisfied?'

'Not really,' I said, because by then I wanted him to stop drinking and I wanted him to want me.

She looked at a line of clocks on the wall and seemed confused. There was one each for about a dozen countries. People in London were going to bed and people in Tokyo were getting up. 'We better catch our bus,' she said. 'It's time for us to get home.'

The way she said *home* meant that it was our home. The one we had made for ourselves without Dad. And it never would be his home. If I was going to see him I'd have to go to his home, wherever that was.

## 14.

# The Patch

A week later Mom and I and Special Ed were sitting in his office with the doctor.

'The results are very promising,' the doctor said, and he smiled. 'They don't tell us anything except that Joey's head is filled with lots of good brains.'

I felt so happy I spoke out of turn. 'Told you so,' I said to Mom. She held a finger up over her puckered lips and gave me a serious look.

The doctor just kept right on going. 'Your problems are not neurologically severe. So it seems the next step is finding the right medication and the right dosage. Presently, I would like to try a transdermal patch. It's like a big round Band-Aid . . .'

When he said 'Band-Aid' my ears perked up.

'. . . that stays on for a day at a time and gives you a steady stream of medication through the skin so that you can avoid the highs and lows you now experience with pills. The goal is to give you a fighting chance to maintain a normal attention span. Once you can do that, then other behaviour therapies, and positive family conditions, can make a significant difference.'

As soon as the doctor said 'family conditions' Mom bit down on her lower lip and uncrossed her legs, pulled down on her skirt, and crossed them the other way. I reached over and squeezed her hand because I knew how it felt to be in trouble.

The doctor and my mom talked for a while and he gave her some papers to read and sign. Then he reached into his case and took out a box. He removed a paper packet from the box, ripped open the edge, and shook out the see-through patch. The first thing I thought was to use markers to make it a cool tattoo.

'Joey,' he said, 'take your shirt off.'

I stood and pulled my T-shirt up and over

my belly and before I had it over my head I heard my Mom gasp. I had taken all the Band-Aids I still had and made the face of a dog on my stomach.

'Don't worry,' the doctor said to Mom. 'It's normal. There's not a kid alive who doesn't like Band-Aids.'

'I want a Chihuahua,' I said, and grinned at Special Ed and he was doing exactly what I thought he'd be doing, which meant my brain was working right. He was trying not to laugh. Last time he was so mad, but now everything was different. Instead of being sick, I was just being a kid. Now that I was getting better, people could like me more.

'We'll try to find one today,' Mom said, and she looked down at her feet because she was a little embarrassed.

'I'm going to put this right on your side,' the doctor said, and he stuck it on and smoothed it down. 'Now, leave it on for twenty-four hours. If you have to take a shower, peel it off, then put it right back on. That's it for now.' He looked up at me and smiled. 'You'll be OK,' he said. 'You're going to be a part of a big test for a new drug that's already worked well for a lot of kids. But let your mom know if you feel dizzy or sick to your stomach and we'll try something else. It's important to get it just right and you are the guy to let us know. We count on you.'

I grinned again and turned to Special Ed. 'If you see me swallowing my house key then you know it's not working,' I said.

'I'll make a note of that,' he replied, and laughed a little bit.

The doctor stood up, and held out his hand. 'Very nice to meet you, Ms Pigza,' he said.

'Likewise,' Mom replied, and she smiled at him in a way that made me think she really liked him. Maybe she is wearing a patch too, I thought, because I hadn't seen Mom look nicely at a man ever.

Then Special Ed said, 'If I can answer any questions or be of any help please let me know.'

'That's very thoughtful of you,' she said.

'I mean it,' he replied, and reached for his wallet. He opened it and pulled out a business card and gave it to her. 'We all want the best for Joey. Call me if you need me.'

She unzipped her bag and slipped the card into an inside pocket. When her hand came back out there was a tissue in it. She turned away from us and pressed it against her eyes. With her other hand she reached for me as if she were searching for something in the dark.

Special Ed opened the door. 'I'll see you tomorrow,' he said to me. 'We still have a few weeks left to work on behaviour and home-work.'

'You bet,' I said.

On the way to the elevator I asked her if she wanted to date the doctor or Special Ed. 'No,' she said, and brushed the idea of it out of the air with her tissue. 'Lord no. You are all the man I can handle,' she said. 'I just like people who like you.' She drew me to her side and I pressed my face against her hip and stayed that way until the elevator opened. Those elevator doors open and close about a million times a day. But when we reached the lobby and they opened for me I felt they had let me out into something new. I just stood there thinking that I was finally going down the right path to being better. That getting better was really happening to me. That it was my turn for everyone to help, and there was no turning back to my old self unless I messed up. And I didn't want to mess up.

'Come on, Joey,' Mom said, and tugged at my arm because the elevator doors began to close. I snapped out of it and stood between the doors and held them open with my arms stretched out like Samson. She ducked under my arm and through and I jumped out right behind her.

'I love elevators,' I said to Mom as we walked towards the bus stop.

'They make me seasick,' she said.

I remembered.

Maybe it was the patch working, or maybe it was what Special Ed had said. He had told me that all my problems were not because I was hyper. 'Some of it is attitude,' he had said. 'If you have a positive attitude things will look a lot better.' And he was right. Because even though I was still Joey Pigza and taking meds and going to a special school for extra help, I didn't feel the same. I felt like Christmas was just a few days away even though it wasn't.

As we walked down the street Mom held up the box of patches the doctor had given her. 'These are *not* Band-Aids,' she said, tapping the box with her fingernail.

'I know the difference,' I said. 'I'm not an

idiot. They took pictures of my brain and I wasn't missing any.'

'Thank God,' Mom said, and started fussing with the hair around my bald spot, and I had to pull her hand away.

'It'll grow back,' I said. 'Don't keep messing with it or I'll put a patch on you.'

'Well, don't pull out your hair and I won't have to mess with it,' she said.

From there we took the bus to a pet store and I had a huge grin on my face because I was right about my Christmas-comes-early feeling. I was smiling up until the moment I found out they didn't have a Chihuahua and were not likely to get one, ever. The pet lady looked at me like I was the only person on the planet who thought a Chihuahua was not a rat.

'They are very nervous,' she explained. 'And they make a yapping noise all day long.'

'That's exactly why I want it,' I replied.

She groaned, then suggested I buy a Rottweiler or a pit bull or some huge dog that looked like the wolf that ate the grandma in Little Red Riding-Hood. I only considered the wolf for a moment because I thought if Grandma returned he could swallow her whole.

'That's only a story,' the pet lady said when I asked if a grandma could be swallowed by a wolf dog.

'Be nice,' Mom whispered to me when the salesperson turned to answer a question from someone else. 'Grandma took care of you when I couldn't.'

I knew that having Grandma swallowed alive wasn't a nice thought and I was trying to be nice like Special Ed and Mom and everyone told me to be. Of course I still love my grandma even after all the awful stuff she did to me, which is scary that you can love someone who is not nice. I guess that is what getting better will do to a person: make you forgive people who have been mean to you.

So we didn't buy any of the dogs and I left really bummed out. But every day while I was still at the downtown special ed we kept checking in the *Thrifty Nickel* free newspaper and finally there was an ad for a half Chihuahua and half dachshund. We called the number and a man brought him over to our house in a shoe box and he was perfect. The dog was great because the Chihuahua half supplied nearly all the good looks except for the really short legs and hot-dog belly, and the dachshund half made him a little less jittery, although he did yap a lot. I named him Pablo. Pablo Pigza. PP for short.

We were destined for each other because right away he decided to sit on the windowsill and wait for me and yap at everyone who went by. Mom said the yapping drives her nuts and that's why she has to turn the TV up really loud, and she has suggested that I take one of my used patches and cut a piece off and stick it on Pablo's belly to see if it would calm him down. 'I don't think so,' I said to her.

'Then snap a rubber band around its snout,' she said. 'That thing is just like you used to be.'

'You loved me then,' I said.

'But I don't have to love that dog,' she replied.

I picked Pablo up by his extra-long belly and held him to her ear and he licked it and tickled her. 'Say you love him,' I said. 'Say it.'

Nobody can resist Pablo. He's just like me. Messed up but lovable.

She caved in. 'OK,' she said. 'I love him too.'

'Don't say it unless you mean it,' I said,

and pressed Pablo's nose back into her ear.

'I love him,' she squealed, and pulled her head away. 'I can't live without him.'

'That's better,' I said. 'Pablo and I feel much better now.'

## 15.

# PictuRE ME HERE

The doctor had said I wouldn't be able to tell that the patch was working, like I could with my old meds. He said it was a different kind of medicine and would take a while to 'kick in.' But, I swear, almost from the first patch I could feel myself winding down like I was on a swing that was slowly stopping. When I told Special Ed this he said it was a good sign because it probably meant I was getting the right dose of medicine at all times and I would no longer have to feel hyper, then feel near dead, then hyper again.

It was great because once I slowed way

down and worked hard at the special-ed centre, everything else seemed to speed up. My last two weeks downtown zipped by quickly, and when I was ready to leave it seemed that not much time had passed but I had changed a lot. Still, not all of me had changed. No matter how smart the doctors are, or no matter what medication I take, I'll always somewhere inside myself be wired wrong and nothing can be done about it. I didn't make my own bed, but it's mine anyway whether I like it or not. And as Special Ed said, 'You gotta face the hand you're dealt and deal with it, and make your problems be the smallest part of who you are.' And he's right.

My friend Charlie was getting ready to go too. He had built up the strength in one of his little hands so that they attached a plastic arm over it and he could control almost real-feeling soft plastic fingers on the end. After Special Ed said my stay was nearly over I found Charlie and he shook my hand with his new one and it was a great moment for me. But it was really great for him.

'Feel this, Pigza,' he said, and he wiggled one of his fingers and tickled the inside of my hand.

'Awesome,' I said. 'When do you get the other?'

'In a few weeks,' he replied. 'I'll let you know.'

'We're the only Pigza in the phone book,' I said. 'Call me and you can come over and meet Pablo.'

He made little dialling motions with his finger. 'Will do,' he said.

Finally Mom and Special Ed met with Mrs Jarzab and Mrs Maxy and they all agreed to let me back as long as I lived by the rules and took my medication. After the meeting, when Mom told me that I said, 'I love rules.' And I did. I even made up dog rules for Pablo because he was chewing up stuff and pooping on the floor and so I had to send him to his own doggy special-ed classes so he could learn to only chew his dog toys and poop in the front yard.

I was really happy that first day back because the special-ed bus didn't stop at my front door any more. I walked to school and when I passed through the front doors I walked down to the office.

'Can I see Mrs Jarzab?' I asked the secretary.

'Welcome back,' she said. 'Have you been on vacation?'

'No,' I replied. 'Remember me? I cut off Maria's nose tip and was sent to the big special-ed centre and got a patch. Wanna see?'

'I think Mrs Jarzab is very busy right now, Joey,' she replied, and reached across her desk and pulled my shirt back down. 'Can I help you with something?'

'I want to say the Pledge of Allegiance over the loudspeaker,' I said. 'I never did that before and now I want to.'

'Well, take a seat,' she said, 'and I'll see what I can do.'

While I was waiting Nurse Holyfield came by. I grinned at her as if I were a squinty Halloween pumpkin with light glowing out of my eyes and ears and mouth, and she grinned right back.

'Don't tell me you are in trouble already?' she said, and propped her hands on her hips.

'No,' I cried out, almost laughing. 'I'm the new and improved Joey.' I lifted my shirt up. 'See this patch?' I said. 'Now watch this.' I put my hands on my lap, and I stared across the room at a painting of a clown with an old shoe for a hat and I didn't move my head an inch in any direction. I didn't even blink.

After about a minute she asked, 'Well? What do you want me to watch?'

'That was it,' I said. 'Just me sitting *still*. Don't you get it? I'm better.'

She smiled. 'How wonderful,' she said. 'But now that you're better I won't see you any more.'

'Oh yes you will,' I said. 'I'll just come to visit. But not to throw up.'

'You do that,' she replied.

The secretary returned and said, 'Yes, Mrs Jarzab says you can say the pledge this morning.'

'Way to go, Joey,' Nurse Holyfield said. She looked up at the big clock. 'Gotta run. Gotta get the meds line set up.'

'Give 'em the patch,' I said. 'It's much better than the pills.'

'I'll see what I can do,' she said, and hurried down the hall.

And before long I was standing at the microphone with my hand over my heart saying, 'I pledge allegiance to the flag . . .' And when I finished I added really loudly, 'My name is Joey Pigza, and I'm *back*!' I wanted to say that everyone's nose was safe and not to worry, but Mrs Jarzab snatched the microphone out of my hand and flicked off the volume. Still, 'I'm back! back! back!' echoed down the hall like a giant's footsteps, and I loved the sound of it.

'Thank you, Mrs Jarzab,' I said as she gave me a cross look.

'Now go see Mrs Howard,' she replied, 'before you are tardy on your first day back.'

The deal that Mrs Jarzab and Special Ed worked out was that I had to go to ordinary-school special ed for a week and prove that I wasn't a danger to myself and everyone on the planet until I got back to Mrs Maxy's class. Plus, as Special Ed said to me, other kids' parents need to know that their kids aren't going to come home chopped to bits. 'Always think of the big picture,' he said to me. 'Think of how everyone else feels too.' I knew what he meant because I had seen with my own eyes how crazy Maria's dad got after I hurt her. My mom would have felt the same way if it was my nose that was cut off.

So, starting back with Mrs Howard was OK with me because I had friends in special ed too. When I went down there Mrs Howard made a big fuss over me.

'Welcome back,' she cried out, and knelt down to give me a hug. 'You did a great job on the pledge.'

The moms were all there, and the special-ed aides and all the kids, and everyone who could turned and looked at me and said different things but they all meant, Great to see you back!

'Now, don't get used to it down here,' Mrs Howard said to me. 'I'll be shipping you upstairs to your usual class in no time.'

'I know,' I said, smiling like a half-moon goon. 'I'm getting a second chance.'

'You're a lucky boy,' she said. 'We all need a second chance.' She showed me my desk and it really made me feel good not to have the rules taped to the top like with Mrs Maxy. Because I knew the rules. It wasn't that I never knew them. It was that I kept forgetting to stick to them.

And Harold was still there. My birthday wish for him had not come true while I was away or he'd be out of that neck brace and wheelchair and we'd be playing football.

Mrs Howard was busy helping some other kids so I just went up to Harold's mom. 'I'm back,' I said. I lifted my shirt and showed her my patch. 'I've got new medicine.'

She was really nice. She put her arms round me and squeezed me tight. 'You give me hope, Joey,' she said. 'If you can do it, then maybe Harold can too, someday.'

And it was amazing to me that she said what she did because I never thought someone would ever point to me and say I gave them hope that someday their kid would be like me. When she told me that, I stood real still and looked her in the eye like Mom taught me. 'Are you sure about that?' I asked.

'Ever since the party,' she said. 'When you blew out the candle for his wish, he has been looking for you.'

I looked over at Harold and he was just blowing little bubbles out of his mouth and I didn't think he would ever get better. But because I got better I wanted him to get better too.

Then she said the nicest thing a non-family person has ever said to me. She said, 'You know, Joey, the medication has helped settle you down, but you have been a good kid all along. You are *naturally* good. I hope you know that about yourself. You have a good heart.'

When she said that, it was as if she had just
blown out all the candles on my cake.
'Thanks,' I said, and I had to half turn away
and wipe my eyes on my shoulder. Then I
walked a little way off as if I was going to do
something else. But instead I slipped the old
photo of me standing still out of my pocket
and rubbed it between my thumb and fore-
finger. I'm not a bad kid, I thought. Then I
went over to the bookshelf and picked out a
book, and since no-one was in the Big Quiet
Chair I climbed up and sat down and began to
read.

the END

# JOEY PIGZA LOSES CONTROL
*Jack Gantos*

*Joey's dad is well and truly wired!*

After months of nagging, Joey Pigza is finally allowed to spend the summer holidays with his dad. But he soon finds out why Mom was so worried. If people think Joey has problems, they should meet his dad!

Joey's dad insists he can cope without medication *and* that Joey can too. Joey *so* wants to believe his dad is right – but Joey remembers just how manic he felt before he got help. Can Joey live life his dad's way – or will the chaos take over?

'Truly memorable' *Booklist*

'Brilliant comic writing tinged with the poignancy of reality.' *Bookseller*

ISBN 0 440 864704